Dear Robot

An Anthology of
Epistolary Science Fiction

EDITED BY KELLY ANN JACOBSON

CONTENTS

ACKNOWLEDGMENTS

I would like to thank Ty Coleman, judge of the *Dear Robot* contest, for dedicating time to this project, as well as Jessica Spotswood, judge of the *Magical* contest, who I so nicely forgot to mention in that book.

Huge thanks also go to Elizabeth Nellums, *Dear Robot*'s first reader, for her incredible editing skills and her big heart.

Last but not least, to my contributors: thank you for not only indulging my crazy idea for an anthology of epistolary science fiction, but for turning that idea into so many great stories. You continuously inspire me with your creativity and brilliance.

1. NICKERSON INTERSTELLAR STUDENT EXCHANGE BEHAVIORAL CONTRACT
by Tara Campbell

DRAFT Behavioral Guidelines for the 2155-2156 Academic Year

Dear Gleeb,

We are so happy that you are part of our family this academic year. We realize you're the only Fronzian here in Michigan, so we'll do our best to keep you from getting too lonely. We're longtime hosts with Nickerson Interstellar Student Exchange! We've hosted students from Pendrian, Mont, Grink and Flarb before, so we have some experience with visitors. But of course that doesn't mean we know everything about *you*, and you're certainly learning about *us* too.

As you know, after our last few discussions with our Nickerson Student Exchange advisor, she recommended that we write down some of the lessons we've all learned from each other over the last couple of months. Experiential learning: that's what educational exchange is all about, after all! This draft is our first shot at the document she recommended, and we welcome your input to make it as clear as possible what we can ask and expect of one another.

The most important "rules" (We don't really like the word "rule." All of these points are mostly guidelines, but these first couple are pretty important.)

1) Open communication is key. Please don't hide your feelings because
    a. we're family now!
       and
    b. we've received an orientation on Fronzian skin patterns, but masking your emotions to colorations that aren't in the pamphlet. This makes us unsure of what you're up to or how we should react. In the future, go ahead and let it all hang out! We don't want any more close calls with the Nickerson Student Exchange emergency phaser, now do we?
2) We'll try not to show our teeth very often, because we know it upsets you. We never realized how often we smile—the wonders of cultural exchange! Please forgive us if we slip up and grin. Just remember: we would never chew off your hair to gain your powers, and neither will anyone else in this community.

Those are the biggies, but here are some other things to note:

Food
1) A simple reminder: the birdcage has bars, the cupboards have doors, and the fridge is cold. Only the second two are for food. Our new parakeet's name is Francis, by the way. He'll be living in your hostsister's room for now.
2) We use our mealpacket recombination appliance to prepare most of our food, and we also have an old-fashioned stove for special dinners, so please do not shoot fire from your hands to cook indoors. We'll try this at a fun backyard cookout on our vintage grill before the weather gets bad. Plus, we should have some of your native dishes back from the biohazard testing facility soon. What a picnic we'll have then!

Etiquette/Manners
1) Please do not read your hostsister's diary. While this may seem like a very convenient way to see what she's thinking, this is not a form of communication we use with each other.

2) Please do not enter your hostsister's room without her permission.
   a. "Enter" means any manner of getting through the door, including flattening yourself and sliding underneath it.
   b. "Without her permission" also means when she is asleep.
   c. "May I come in?" or "Please let me in," are acceptable ways to ask for permission, but not when paired with "or I will burn down the door with my handfire." That's not considered polite here in Michigan.

Bathroom/Grooming

1) Please use the drain cover when showering. We don't have another plumber's visit in our hosting budget this year. ☺
2) We are fine with your using the vacuum to brush your hair. Please just clean out the vacuum canister after grooming. (Cultural question: So you only lose your powers if someone *chews off* your hair? Is this why you don't worry about us getting into the vacuum and eating it?)
3) We realize that your people are heavily into bio-recycling, but in this house, the bathroom is the only proper place for bodily waste.
4) We appreciate your eagerness to contribute to the household, but your hostfather doesn't need any help shaving. Neither does your hostsister. Your hostmother is feeling left out, ha ha! Joke.
5) We'll denote "jokes" by signing the letter "j" instead of smiling.

Community

1) We have a roomy house and a nice, big backyard with high fences. This large layout is perfect for us to relax in, and we hope you like it too because our neighbors don't have as much experience with visitors as we do.
2) If you encounter a neighbor, disregard any teeth they may show you (see item 2 of "Most important rules" above).
3) Please do not use hand fire with the neighbors, unless you've been invited for a barbeque. "j"

Next Steps

Once you have a chance to look at this document and discuss any changes with us, we'll send a final, signed copy to our Nickerson Student Exchange advisor. She'll make sure the organization passes along a copy to your parent. We so enjoyed the opportunity to meet him/her (English is so awkward, isn't it?) last week—what an exciting surprise to have a visit from an Ambassador from the Central Galaxies! We know s/he is busy, however, and surely doesn't have time to keep transporting out here to the Milky Way. We hope that you will approach us or your Nickerson Student Exchange advisor first with any additional questions you may have or challenges you may face this year.

Once again, Gleeb, welcome to Earth and to Michigan. We look forward to the rest of the year, and all the other discoveries it will bring!

Signatures

_____   _____

Gleeb (Student)   Date

_____   _____

Frank Lindermann (Hostfather) Date

_____   _____

Betty Lindermann (Hostmother) Date

_____   _____

Margie Lindermann (Hostsister) Date

2. GOD ARTICLE
by Rafael S.W

For a long time I've loved not even you. This no doubt comes as a shock, but are you as surprised as you expected to be? There is none of that gut-sinking, ground up from under, world crashing, what? I know you. At least, I know *this*. We have been poorly-made partners for quite some time. Naturally, of course, this was what first drew me to you. Your tininess, the way you moved quickly through rooms. And you know I appreciated that, me of the ponderous bulk and several million dollars' worth of stolidness behind me. I pretend wealth means nothing, but it helps me at least start up conversations. And I need all the help I can get in the social department, seeing as I've been sitting in the one place for so long people stop their cars and have children stand next to me for a photo. I get a gut ache just seeing a Toyota Corolla slowly drawing to a halt. But I should stop complaining. You've had your fill of my big belly. Let's talk about this, us. I had the backing of universities, you had the support of space.

Maybe this is why I loved you—your defiance of traditional models. The rules that governed the rest of us didn't seem to apply to you. No one would go so far as to call you unstable, though that would be entirely fair. It's strange when I think of you in that way. That someone I associate with such fierce passion decays into other particles the second you're seen. This is perhaps another reason why we were so terrible at parties. I still remember Vladivostok in '72, where we got lightly obliviated on tequila. You were sitting in a corner telling anyone who would listen about your Mexican hat, which you swore had nonzero strength but which looked like something you'd bought at the second-hand shop down the road. I tried to catch your eye that night, but had been engaged in my own kind of self-destruction. My ex was in the room just down the hall, with a young Japanese researcher famous for his knowledge on Yukawa couplings. I'd been considering calling in a bomb threat just so that I would have some chance at interrupting them. I didn't, of course, being born an irrevocable coward. Instead I loitered aggressively in the kitchen. In the lounge people raised their glasses. Was it the new year? Was it the end of humanity? When I next looked back you were gone. This proved, more than anything else, your skill with otherwise empty space.

It wasn't until many years later that we were thrown together. I had been searching for you, as had plenty of other people of course, but who cares about them? But it was a casual kind of search, like looking for a lost Tasmanian tiger. I knew there was something missing in my life, but it wasn't necessarily your absence that explained it. I would hold my bedsheet high at night, imagine it as a model for the universe. You here, somewhere on my wide white galaxy, well that would be nice. It would explain a lot. But let's not pretend I spent the intervening years pining. I was making my own way, discovering all kinds of rare and flighty beings who would make my mile-long intestines ache but would leave me hollow. I made a certain name for myself, which you will do me the courtesy of not enquiring about. It is not something I am proud of, but there aren't many better ways of biding my time. I was looking for you. Even when the rest of the world was sleeping, I would craft a thousand ingenious plans for bringing about our collision. And then one day, I did.

We were a match made in factories—the kind of future-embracing that all scientists are rushing to do. Our chaperones had won Nobel prizes, their search for intelligence fueled by an endless lust for more intelligence. I've got a hundred brilliant scientist friends, but just like the dorky schoolchildren they'd been, all they could do was talk about you. I wanted to *meet* you. From all their conversations, I felt like I already had. This was way back when, before the obsessions and apocalyptic naysayers came round to protest our love. Before the newspapers cried out that there was something perverse, even *dangerous*, about our coupling. Even if we didn't believe them, I would come to lower my gaze in the town, and you would revert to using your double-barrelled maiden name. Had we known that would be the result, would we still have gone ahead with things the way we did? Of course. Neither of us are daft enough to believe that there is any free will in the universe.

The first real night we spent together, I split you in two. This was not in a bad way, but nor did it create a black hole and destroy the universe, so I guess it counts as a success. We were a little clumsy, as befits our failures of supersymmetry. All that nonsense about coming from a rib, baby you came straight from God himself. I'd heard rumours about you giving weight to things, but our coupling (or uncoupling) was the first time the act had held meaning for me. In the past I'd gone through the routine of bringing some particles home and just seeing what happened. But with you it felt like we were creating history. I don't like to brag, but when we accelerated it was almost at the speed of light. People talk about sex toys but I humbly suggest that with 11,000 revolutions per second, I might be the preferred option in the bedroom. Oh darling. All this talk is making me hot. Gosh how long has it been since our first big bang? Want to go again?

As you can probably guess, I'm drunk. This should make you disgusted, but in this way isn't it consistent with all worthwhile knowledge? It either makes you awestruck or revolted. If it's any consolation I'm drunk not on brandy nor goon but emptiness. Perhaps this makes no difference to your rightful revulsion, but I offer only this. I have been so goddamn lonely since we decided to split. It doesn't matter that I said we'd be better off. We're complex enough creations that we can be both better off and more miserable at the same time.

It would be fair for you to wonder why, with all this love that you've heard from me, that a breakup is the answer. But here's the thing. You have eclipsed me. Go on, laugh. Almost thirty k's wide, and 100 meters deep, and I'm feeling emasculated by something subatomic. But that's how it is. When I love you, I am nothing but my love for you. A vessel for your existence. Already I cannot imagine a life without you, but I must. Just knowing you are real and out there is enough for me.

3. WHO DO YOU THINK YOU ARE
by Misha Herwin

Dear Robot,

Given our history, I hardly like to call you this. I'm not sure that "Mother" or "Mom" would be appropriate either. All I know is that thirty one years ago I was one of your first hatchlings. I don't suppose that you would remember—there must have been so many of us since then—but if by any chance you have any data stored in your memory banks about me, Marcie Blake, serial no. Kid207/15/A, then I would be very glad to hear from you.

Yours (kind of),
Marcie

—

Dear Marcie,

You are correct. My memory banks are not designed to store data of individual hatchlings. You, however, were the template for all the others and information about the method of inception, gestation, and subsequent production of designated hatchlings is available in the Mendlesohnian Archives. The Mater Project is now in the public domain and can be accessed with Code ALICE/Kid207/15/A.

Alice

Dear Alice,

You have a name! I've often wondered. When I was little I asked my mom about you, but she said she didn't know anything. Is that true? Were the biological parents really not told?

Yours,
Marcie

—

Dear Marcie,

There is no interaction between Maters, of which I am the prototype and the providers of the embryos.

Back in the day however, in the beginning there was @@@@@@@@@@@@

—

Alice!

There was what? I need to know. I accessed the records held in the archives, but there was nothing specific about you and me.

—

Dear Marcie,

Data deleted. Check online Code ALICE/MaterProject/Kid207/ 15/A. Be careful where you tread.

Alice

—

Dear Alice,

I found it. Not where you said, but down the WormHole. It's amazing what you can find on that site. It might not be legal, at least not quite legal, but we all use it for all sorts of family things. To be honest, I don't know why I didn't look there first.

No. Scrap that, I do know. I actually wanted to make contact with you. I wanted to find out exactly where I came from, because I don't believe that the place where I spent the first nine months of my existence didn't have any effect on me at all.

Yours,
Marcie

—

Dear Marcie,

Please in-put data. I too would like to know, to remember…

—

Alice,

OK, here it is. Not very scientific, or even necessarily accurate, WormHole doesn't work like that, but it's all I could find.

The Mater Project: Conceived, hey guys there's a good one!!! ☺ ☺ ☺ by Prof. Amalie Whitestone. Funded by the government, ongoing, as a way of getting alpha females to reproduce. No hassle, morning sickness, swollen ankles, or stretch marks. Pop down to your local fertility clinic, state preference as boy or girl, shed an egg or two, get your chosen mate to donate, and KEBAM, nine months later lift the hatch and take out your perfect BABY.

First kid podded. Marcie Blake. Parents: Andrea Blake, particle physicist. Dominic Cavanagh, solar flare specialist with OUEP. The guys that go off to explore other universes.

Robotmom: Alice, first successful wholly artificial womb. Looks like, feels like, works like a real woman.

Is that true, Alice? Do you look real? I couldn't find an image of you, but when I screw up my eyes and concentrate really hard, I kind of remember…something.

Marcie x

—

Dear Marcie,

…bright lights … voices… "It's taken. We've done it." High fives. Then tubes and monitors and screens and … a tiny moving image. "See her toes, her fingers. Hear her heart beat."

"Cool." "Awesome." "Do we go public yet?" "And the mom, the real mom, what does she think?"

You kick. You swim in your warm bath of amniotic fluid. You suck your thumb. I see it all. I sit and watch and wait. And then…

Alice x

—

And then? Oh please Alice what happened next? Did my mom come and check up on me? Did she and my dad visit lots?

Marcie xx

—

Dear Marcie,

I had no visitors. There was only you and me and the music. It was embedded in my synapsis, as the words were too. As you got bigger, I spoke them out loud and I listened to the beating of your heart and the beating of mine.

Alice xx

—

Dear Alice,

You have a heart? I can't get my head round this. But on one level it makes sense a baby needs to hear its mother's heartbeat. I guess that's why they factored it in.

Love,
Marcie xxx

—

Dear Marcie,

Hand over delayed. Parents fail to keep appointment.

Alice x

—

Dear Alice,

We seem to have lost contact. My mail is getting bounced back. It must be something to do with the server. I can't get down the WormHole either and just when it was all beginning to make sense, of a sort.

Feeling very frustrated and missing our e-mails,

Love,
Marcie xxx

PS. I've attached a news item. Think it must be about us. Found it on a derelict site when I was surfing.

"Hell fire will destroy their work," says Pastor. "Scientists will burn for all eternity. Their sins will be purged. Nature must not be perverted." A group calling itself Sons of the Earth stormed the Mendelsohn Institute last night in protest against Professor Amalie Whitestone's groundbreaking work in artificial gestation. During the subsequent gun battle one of the experimental maters went missing. The robot was later discovered on the banks of the Eden. Official sources say that no harm came to the baby.

—

Dear Marcie,

I terminate tomorrow. My usefulness is over. I am unravelling. Images flit across my vision. I see a ribbon of water. There are trees. Sky. I sit on grass. I hold you. You wriggle and gurgle and smile up at me. I, programmed to respond, smile back. They are looking for us. The professor wants me back. You too. You have been with us too long. Tomorrow Andrea Blake will come for you.

I kept you safe. When they came to destroy us, I kept you safe. I kept you…

Love Alice xxxx
—

Dear Alice,

I know you won't get this. Stupidly I started this all too late and now I don't suppose I will ever know the whole truth. Whatever it is and whatever they do to out of date robots who have outlived their uses,

I will never forget you.

Lots of love and thanks,
Marcie xxxx

PS You are going to be a grandma.

4. DRINK, KILL, CONTRACT
by Michelle Vider

TASK TODAY: INTERPRET THIS CONVERSATION [SEE TRANSCRIPT]

Supervisor Rebecca introduced me to two ESA researchers and potential astronauts (Lora Sayer, Malcolm Halley) who wanted to talk about space and their rare genetic disorder. Their extreme photosensitivity relates to my specific area of astrobiology research.

>Treat us as if we're vampires, Lora said. The same sun avoidance applies.

>What if we *were* vampires, Mal said.

<I asked, What?

>Dr. Harker, he said. Jo, he added.

(I'll give them this: I actually liked them. Visiting researchers usually storm in with their entitlement and outrageous demands for everyday drones like me, but Lora and Mal *made an appointment*. They even kept the introductory "Jo is short for... Joanna? Jonathan? Neither, then, wonderful," to under ten seconds before we got to work.)

What would change, Mal asked, if I said we were vampires?

<Just about everything. We would—you would be *vampires*, first of all, and *in space*, with no—

>You'd be with us, he said.

<I beg your FUCKING pardon.

>You could use our bodies to analyze solar radiation on the human body in varying sensitivities, he said. And we would need your body to keep us alive.

<And you're just done with this conversation, I said to Lora.
>I'm observing, Lora said. He's not wrong.
>Haven't you wanted to go to space? Mal asked. Haven't you wanted to go as much as we have?

I left the room and apparently swore loudly enough to have our ESA HR rep and Neil DeGrasse Tyson scold me for doing so in front of a visiting school group. I didn't mention the vampires in the conference room.

\#

TASK TODAY: COMPLETELY ABANDON LIFE'S WORK BECAUSE VAMPIRES

>**Life's work so far**: understand solar radiation as it affects the bodies of living things in this solar system.

>**Revolutionary work adjacent to life's work:** understand two chemosynthetic humanoid lifeforms who would gladly unlock the secret of living without sunlight, voluntarily shipping themselves off into space, at the price of my blood.

>>Like the literal drinking of blood from my body.

>>Unlock the secrets of human immortality and only cost would be use of my physical body.

>>>Parasitic chemosynthetic humanoids (previously known in journal as COLLEAGUES Lora Sayer and Malcolm Halley) at least offered courtesy of consent re: my bodily autonomy.

>>>>How long would that bodily autonomy thing last if we shared this with anyone else? How long would it take the normally sane scientific community to devolve into rampant unchecked human experimentation when this was dangled in front of them?

>>Is it chemosynthetic if they still require oxygen but not light, and they ALSO require metals, proteins, glucose available in the blood and its plasma?

>Am I really doing this?

\#

TASK TODAY: APOLOGIZE TO VAMPIRE-COLLEAGUES

<I apologized.
>They accepted.
<We agreed to work on clarifying objectives.
\#

TASKS THIS WEEK: CLARIFY, ORGANIZE, REWORK OBJECTIVES

>How.............................

>>I got nothing.

\#

BRAINSTORM: TRANSCRIPT EXCERPT OF MEETING WITH JO HARKER (SELF), LORA SAYER, AND MALCOLM HALLEY

<Problem with space, I said. No one can go to space alone. No one can *get* to space alone. Space requires so much communal effort, enough hands involved that the shuttle might as well be pushed up and out solely by the support of all those hands.

>No secrets in space, Lora said.

>What a bore, Mal said. That's why everyone loses their goddamn minds up there. Not that we would. Probably.

<Maybe we can start by making your vampirism seem less like *fucking vampirism* and more like a metabolic anomaly, I said.

>There's no difference, if you think about it, she said.

<God, I know that—*now* I know that—but we have to—I don't know.

>I have a synthetic formula that would spare you some of the work, she said.

<And *why* didn't you mention that before? I asked.

>She just revealed the greatest secret of our lives to you and— Lora interrupted Mal.

>We wanted to see if we could rely on you, Lora said.

<Why, I asked. Why do you want to go to space?

>We seem fortunate to have our strength and immortality, she said. But for centuries, even longer for me, we've been locked in our houses, locked to the earth, this place that would kill us if it had the chance.

<I know it's been a while, but welcome back to the land of the living, I said. For you, the sun is a threat; for the rest of us, it's guns or the capitalism-and-austerity hit squad.

>So let's get out of here, Mal said.

\#

FOLLOWUP NOTES: SERIOUSLY, THOSE OBJECTIVES

>Fuck the search for a Goldilocks planet. What if we could adapt

our bodies to a chemosynthetic metabolism?

>>What if we could adapt our bodies to the dominant minerals and chemicals of the planets available to us? Adapt to the *Star Trek* idea of human<u>oid</u>, not human but a *type* of creature, a blueprint with infinite diversity in infinite combinations.

>How to explain to the ESA and the entire scientific community that two of these humanoids exist in the world and could unlock the secret of translating and exporting human biology to any planet in the solar system?

\#

MEETING SUMMARY: CATCHING UP WITH LORA AND MALCOLM

>Neither opposed to sequencing DNA to discover the elements that triggered their changes from human to humanoid.

>>**NB:** Both Lora AND Mal would have to be sequenced and compared; Lora was transformed millennia before Malcolm—what would that reveal? (Sidenote: MILLENNIA????)

>Lora shared recipe/formula for their synthetic blood cocktail, with condition that I would organic chem that shit to make it more potent/effective, entirely transition them away from human blood.

>>Mal: "Keep the copper taste, though. It's so good."

Lora: "Are you helping or hurting?"

Mal: "But see how adorable Jo looks when they're shocked—how can you resist that face?"

\#

PERSONAL NOTES FOR THERAPY JOURNAL (I NEED TO GO BACK TO THERAPY LIKE RIGHT NOW)

-Why am I not more freaked out at the total disruption and subversion of everything I know to be true?

-Why does this supernatural condition, known throughout human history as something terrifying, suddenly appear before me as something *not* terrifying that can fit into existing paradigms of disease and disorder?

-Why have I suddenly developed the self-preservation instincts of—what's that animal that became extinct when sailors landed on its territory and it was so adorable and trusting and delicious that it became extinct in about 10 minutes? I think it was Australian? It was like a dodo, but a mammal, and adorable, like me, like I am a mammal and adorable and they're going to *devour me*, literally, when I only wanted that sexually at first?

-What are the psychiatric effects of sexual attraction to project colleagues who have suddenly revealed themselves to be supernatural predators out of legend oh god it just sounds hotter when I put it like that.

DELETE THIS, YOU FUCKING MESS

#

NEW OBJECTIVE: THE TRUTH? HAS IT COME TO THIS?

>I am a scientist. I search for facts.

>>I use those facts to create theories, and those theories to create stories, and those stories to generate interest, and that interest to generate money, because this is our capitalist dystopia where exploration for its own sake has no value and we are nothing without money and we have no money without interest. (Did I make a pun?)

>When I say "we should tell them the truth about the vampirism" I don't mean *let's tell them the truth about vampirism*.

>>I mean let's write a paper that can be headlined in the popular media SCIENTISTS DISCOVER REAL-LIFE VAMPIRES, then back up this sensationalist nonsense with very boring science, and then reveal our crackpot idea to get into space to discover the biological blueprint of humanoid life, one that wouldn't utilize the precise heat of our local star to exist, but could thrive on other elements found in large quantities on other worlds.

>>A metabolic disorder (something about the word *metabolic* instantly sends people to sleep) that could actually be the key to life itself.

>>And (because we're not mentioning *the immortal vampire thing*) the subjects plus self must be rushed into space before they die.

>Lora is literally thousands of years old. Yes, Malcolm Halley is related to *those* Halleys, the ones with everything in goddamned England named after them for discovering that orbital trajectories could be measured and mapped.

<So I'll take this grand conclusion to them for their input.

#

TRANSCRIPT (EXCERPT) (SLIGHTLY EDITORIALIZED)

<So what if we wrote a paper and proposal to get us to space and we told the scientific community something like the truth? I asked.

24

>You're coming with us? asked Mal.

<(PANIC PANIC PANIC) Yes if you still want me to?

>We do, Lora said.

>The truth? Lora asked.

<Not all of it, I said. Once we analyze your genes, I'll have to—I don't know—see if there are any markers that would blow the whole thing up by revealing the etiology. Ideally, we could sell it as a disorder, not a disease—a disorder we can induce and control, not a disease that can be contracted.

>Seems like a matter of word choice there, champ, Mal said. Just use one and not the other.

<(terrible hollow gurgling sound of frustration) No, it's not that simple.

>Actually, it is, Lora said. But we can't show you here.

>Our place, then, Mal said.

<What, NOW?

He shrugged, she said seven, he texted me the address, and I am having dinner with earth's future vampire astronauts.

#

PERSONAL NOTES ON DINNER

-Well fuck my life, it's officially a disease.

--Which is something I knew because Lora had mentioned how she had CONTRACTED the condition, but I was in denial and it's a DISEASE.

---Contracted from venom.

-Three types of bites: to drink, to kill, to contract.

--Glands look almost invisible inside the mouth, behind upper and lower canines, glands that consciously swell up and release with pressure.

---*That* intimate, and it was only cocktail hour.

-Venom causes total physical transformation.

-Memory for immortals seems a tricky thing. Lora's memory has been stretched so thin that she can barely pick one specific century out from another. Mal is younger and remembers whole decades like years.

--Both remember transforming, adjusting, isolation, attempts at community, but mostly isolation, until they found each other in 1750s.

-How many like them in the world? Lora thinks <100. Largest

community she's lived in numbered no more than 20, due to extreme demand on resources.

-Does anyone know about their work with the synthetic?

--Some in their community know about their open scientific work, but they're very distant from them. Mal has never lived among them; Lora hasn't since hahahahahahaha if I type it then it's real and I hate myself and what I've become.

-I slept over. I slept. Yes.

#

TASKS THIS WEEK

>Schedule Lora and Mal's supervised blood donation.

>>Find one trusted confidential witness. WHO? Why don't I have friends? Or a solicitor?

>Schedule full genome sequencing and analysis.

>>Who's paying for this?? Schedule first, ask later. I feel like anything's possible at this point. I'm a chemist and an astrobiologist working with people who have metabolic anomalies that can transform humans into the most adaptable species that has ever, or could ever, exist. Anything's possible. Literally anything.

>>>**Confidentiality**. Find a solicitor to draft NDAs! Are the commercial sequencing techs already bound by those? How much is an NDA worth? Why can't I think anymore?

>Remember space? We're doing this to get into space.

>>NASA hints at manned missions to Mars in 2030s—could it take that long? Could it be that soon? I forget how time works now.

>>>They're patient. I'm unmoored.

#

(PERSONAL) THE OTHER SHOE DROPPED

Blood donation scheduled for today. Lora and Mal never showed. I had a solicitor and witness and the tech and they seemed very disappointed in me.

I like to think this is my rational mind speaking, but it's more likely self-loathing. *Anyway*. It's so utterly unlikely that the greatest discovery in human biology should be dropped into my lap and that I should actually be allowed to follow it to its logical conclusion. Jo Harker, my dear and only self, have you met the scientific method? Its entire existence, as a method, is to stop these leaps in knowledge from happening, because a leap is often so large that it's hard to tell where one lands, how one got there, and how others can follow. It's not a discovery if no one else can follow.

But that's why we were starting with the supervised donation and full genome sequencing! Why I chose a lab to perform the sequencing and made sure to have a solicitor draft an addendum to our contract including a very large, very terrifying paragraph on chain of custody so the blood samples provided were never unaccounted for, never handled by more than two people per sample, never compromised.

\#

(PERSONAL) OK MAYBE I'M ALSO TERRIBLE

I went to their house and they were gone.

Maybe I should have gone sooner? The day they failed to show, I called and texted, but should I have made a larger statement? Should I have run out of the building, run the whole way to their house (more realistically: called a cab, waited for cab, taken cab, arrived there, appear handsomely out of breath for dramatic reasons)—

Should I have told them it didn't matter, it was all right if they didn't want to do this, this was so much bigger than all of us, so much bigger than—than humanity itself. It seemed worth it, even if we couldn't carry it out to its fullest conclusion, because I had met them, known them, learned this incredible story, and even if none of us ever reach space, we've reached some Jane Austenish understanding of ourselves and each other. Maybe we should part ways, civilly, or maybe we could continue to be just the way we are, and that would be all right, too.

That would have been good and interesting, so I didn't do it. Instead, I waited five days and then went to their house and saw it was empty.

Not empty of things, just people. Empty of significant things. I don't know how to explain that feeling, of a house that was once full and now feels conspicuously empty of people. It's not any one thing that designates it empty.

I didn't see a note in any obvious place.

I think the door had been forced.

\#

TASKS THIS WEEK: NEW TO-DO LIST, OLD OBJECTIVES

>I started this new offshoot project journal when Lora and Mal came to me because I thought it would need its own separate space,

and it did. Now I have to return to what I was doing and none of it looks like language anymore. Something about acids and radiation and things that seemed interesting just a short while ago and now nothing does.

>Should I burn this? Scan it, save it, encrypt it, then burn it? What do I do when this seems bizarre enough to be fic

\#

NEW OBJECTIVES: ADJUST TO IMMORTALITY

>Yes it bothers me that Mal didn't even let me finish writing the word *fiction* before he and Lora surprised me by breaking into my apartment and my bedroom.

SUMMARY:

>Apparently the wider vampire community isn't as isolated as previously believed.

>>Since they discovered the plan I had developed with Lora and Mal[1]

>>> I can stay here and wait for the conservative vampire hit squad[2]

>>>>Or I could leave civilization with them

>>>>>In exchange Lora has offered to turn me, since our mutual curiosity in merging our species has led to a price on our heads.

>I took my notebooks and left my laptop wiping its hard drive, and I even had time to pack a toothbrush and facewash because the world is large enough to hide in and that doesn't mean we have to be without the basics.

>And now I live out in the world with them.

>And turning has hurt.

>>I'll likely never be outside again, but the sun was just going to give me cancer anyway so there's no huge loss there.

>>>Strangely unattached to my life's work now that I'm dead.

\#

TASKS THIS WEEK: BUILDING A NEW LIFE!

---

[1] Unsurprising: they weren't the only two adjacent to the community to have scientific interests! And legal interests! In the end, NDAs and attorney-client privilege are worth nothing. Good to know.

[2] I'm so bad at this, honestly, I hated *Tinker Tailor Soldier Spy*, I don't understand how our world governments are run by people who don't believe in the power of a good well-written memo to clear things up in the murky field of international relations.

>Simplify recipe for synthetic blood cocktail, now that Lora and Mal have a genuine chemist with them. (It's me!)

>>And remove that copper taste, or make a separate flavor extract so Mal can add that in himself, I don't care how goddamned authentic it tastes.

>Find a new therapist who takes cash (HAHA ALL OF THEM)

>>(I really need to talk this out with someone, preferably someone board certified who is not adjacent to the vampire hit squad, so maybe wait until we're in another country and Lora has had time to stalk a few candidates and their habits.)

>Start stockpiling various cash currencies.

>Learn credit card fraud?

>Science off the grid?

>>Apparently there's significant demand for off-the-grid chemists and physicians, so once my body has finished tearing itself apart and adjusting to its new mutated form, I should look into an off-the-books MD. Maybe someday I'll have a lab again.

>Plan trip to Antarctica for sometime in May through July.

>>24 hours of night at the pole, astronomical twilight in the penguin parts. Total body coverage needed anyway due to appearing human and extreme cold having that sort of effect on normal human skin, so that's convenient for us. I've heard good things about Antarctica.

>Never worry about grant writing again.

>Enjoy the afterlife.

5. FUN(DRAISING) WITH METEOROIDS
by Sarena Ulibarri

Dear Mr. Kohler,

Greetings from NASA! We are pleased to offer you a rare opportunity.

The NASA Near Earth Object program tracks both large and small objects such as asteroids, meteoroids and comets. While larger objects can be more dangerous, if the trajectory of smaller objects poses a threat to any occupied areas, we are able to remove the object before it enters Earth's atmosphere. Over the next decade, we estimate that this will save millions of dollars of structural damage.

As part of our newest fundraising and public awareness campaign, we have decided to deliver the original meteoroids to the individuals or organizations that would have been most affected by their impact. According to our calculations, the meteoroid now in your possession would likely have struck your domicile on March 23rd between 9:00 pm and 10:00 pm CST.

Below, you will find a donation form and a return label. Please, if you would like to keep the meteoroid, send a check to the address below for any amount you are able. All donations will assist the Near Earth Object program in its continued efforts to monitor and remove dangerous objects before they impact Earth. If you are unable to make a donation, or prefer not to keep the meteoroid, simply affix the return label to the box and take it to any USPS drop-off location.

For more information about the Near Earth Object program and this campaign, please visit nasacorp.com/neo/public.

Sincerely,
Victoria Siskind
NEO Public Awareness Manager

—

Dear NASA People,

Thanks for the big-ass weird rock, but, no, I will not be sending you a donation. I will also not be returning the rock. Because, really? Who exactly thought this was a good idea?

A) Your donation amounts on the included slip are all in multiples of $1000. You know what I do for a living? I install carpets in office buildings. It's a job that requires a lot of heavy lifting and doesn't pay enough for me to have thousands of extra dollars lying around to donate to harebrained science projects.

B) The box is broken, because that is one freaking heavy rock. I'd think your engineers would have figured out something more heavy-duty than cardboard to mail it in. I now have a very awkward, basketball-sized doorstopper, which, hey, I kinda needed a doorstopper anyway, so your efforts haven't gone completely to waste.

C) This whole thing smells like a scam. Since when does NASA need money from dudes like me? And don't these meteorites or whatever burn up in the atmosphere? This doesn't exactly look like it would have caused Armageddon. If it really was on target for my house, I don't know that it would have done much damage. Knocked out a window maybe, or put a hole in the wall. This house already has a few of those thanks to some of my drunk friends. Probably it would have been nothing more than a sprinkle of ashes on my roof.

D) If this is not a scam, I'm pretty sure it's an elaborate prank to punish me for not going to some lame star-gazing party with my girlfriend. So, ha ha Makayla, but you're not tricking me into forking over money for that telescope you wanted.

So, whether this is real or not, please, just add me to whatever the mail equivalent is of your "Do Not Call" list.

Sincerely,
Chad Kohler
—

Dear Mr. Kohler,

Thank you for your feedback about NASA's new Near Earth Object public awareness campaign. We urge you to reconsider a donation, and have included an updated donation form with more flexible options. Every contribution, however small, helps us toward our goal of advancing aerospace technologies.

If you are still unable to contribute, please return the meteoroid using the included postage-paid return label. If the meteoroid is not valuable to you, it may be valuable to a museum collection or other scientific agencies. This is a limited time offer; please respond ASAP.

Very Respectfully,
Vicky Siskind
NEO Public Awareness Manager

—

From: kohler.c.227@memail.com
To: siskvic@nasa.com
Subject: Space Rock Junk

Dear Siskind and Co.,

I'm not wasting a stamp on this, and I guess you conveniently forgot to include that "included postage-paid return label," so thanks for having your contact info on your quasi-legit-looking website.

I cannot emphasize enough how much I simply DO NOT CARE about space junk. My girlfriend is always going on about how scientists discovered some new planet fifty million light years away and it annoys the crap out of me. I've got a mortgage, I've got root canals, I've got a bum back from too much heavy lifting. I've got *Earth* problems. What the hell do I need to know about some galaxy I'll never see?

So, I have reconsidered your offer, and the answer is still no. The space rock now has a fulfilling career as a doorstopper. What are you going to do, send some astronauts to break into my house and steal it back? Actually, please do—it's starting to chip the paint on my door.

Thanks,
Chad Kohler

—

From: siskvic@nasa.com
To: kohler.c.227@memail.com
Subject: Re: Space Rock Junk
[Download Attachment]

Dear Mr. Kohler,

Although I understand your skepticism, I can assure you that we are a perfectly legitimate organization, though we have stumbled upon financial difficulties. For many years, NASA has worked with a number of private companies to assist our efforts toward both manned and robotic spaceflight. It was only a year ago, however, that we lost government funding and became a completely privatized entity. This, as you can imagine, has forced us to develop more creative funding solutions.

The work we do is incredibly important for the safety of Earth. Small objects such as the one in your possession can cause localized damage, but the NEO program is more concerned with extinction-level impacts. One of these large objects could be on its way here right now, but if we don't have enough funding, we can't see it coming or do anything to stop it.

Attached, you will find a donation form that you may print out and mail along with your contribution to the NASAcorp.com™ Near Earth Orbit program at your convenience. We will also accept PayBud or iPay.

Sincerely,
Vicky Siskind

—

From: kohler.c.227@memail.com
To: siskvic@nasa.com
Subject: Re: Re: Space Rock Junk

Don't waste your scare tactics on me. I'm still not sending you scammers any money.

Chad

—

From: siskvic@nasa.com
To: kohler.c.227@memail.com
Subject: Re: Re: Re: Space Rock Junk

Chad,

Listen, I get it. To be honest, I fought against this campaign, and so far we haven't received a single positive response. I knew it was a bad idea when the memo was titled "Fun(draising) with Meteoroids." I was just impressed they got the term "meteoroid" right.

Because here's the deal: the company that bought us knows nothing about aerospace technologies. Nor do they seem to actually know much about running a successful business, which I thought was the whole point of going private. A couple of their (numerous) CEOs used to work for one of those mail-order compact disc sellers, where they sent CDs in the mail and you had to pay to keep them or else send them back. Hence, their current brilliant scheme. Machines that were meant to be mining asteroids have been repurposed as orbital vacuum cleaners for Near Earth Objects like the one we sent you.

For what it's worth, the meteoroid currently in your possession really did pose a threat to your specific GPS coordinates. Hundreds of these things whiz by us all the time. Thousands. Earth is like a giant dart board and most of the universe has pretty bad aim. But now and then, one hits a bullseye. Even the small ones—the basketball-sized ones—can do some serious damage.

So, there's that. Enjoy your doorstopper.

Vicky S.

——

From: kohler.c. 227@memail.com
To: siskvic@nasa.com
Subject: Re: Re: Re: Re: Space Rock Junk

Vicky,

I've had the weirdest couple of days. I guess I really started to believe that the rock could have been an actual threat. If it had hit, my living room would be smoldering crater right now.

After I read your email, I went out onto the porch to smoke a cigarette. I've lived in this house for three years and probably smoked a thousand cigarettes out there, but this might be the first time I've looked at the sky. You can't really see the stars here. The whole universe is hidden behind city lights and pollution.

I started wondering if my insurance covers meteorite damage (I looked it up later, it doesn't), and then I started thinking about that date and time you said in the first letter: March 23rd between 9pm and 10pm. I was supposed to be out with my girlfriend that night, but we'd gotten into a fight and I'd ditched her to go home and play video games. I'd have been inside that smoldering crater when it hit. Man, I just don't even know what to do with that information. I stopped using the rock as a doorstop and rolled it into a closet because I didn't want to think about it every time I walk in the door. But it didn't work. I'm thinking about it all the time.

Chad

—

To: kohler.c.227@memail.com
From: management@nasa.com
Subject: Re: FW: Re: Re: Re: Re: Space Rock Junk

Dear Mr. Kohler,

We regret to inform you that your correspondence cannot be delivered to the intended recipient, as this individual is no longer an employee of NASAcorp.com™.

It has come to our attention that you received your Fundstarter campaign backer's reward—Original Meteoroid Material—before we were able to process your payment. Please click this link to resubmit your payment information.

We appreciate your business. Thank you for helping us keep the skies clear.

Kind Regards,
John Lindsey
NEO Public Awareness Manager

—

From: kohler.c.227@memail.com
To: management@nasa.com
Subject : Re: Re: FW: Re: Re: Re: Re: Space Rock Junk

No! I never backed any kind of crowdfunding campaign for you jerks, and if I had, I certainly wouldn't have asked you to send me a rock. Oh, and I looked up your Fundstarter campaign. It didn't even meet its goal! How are you trying to collect payments from me when you didn't even collect payments from the people who legitimately pledged?

Also, pretty weird how your story keeps changing. Seriously, don't email me again.

Chad

—

From: connections@linkup.net
To: vicky.siskind@memail.com
Subject: Chad Kohler would like to connect with you!

Chad Kohler, laborer at Big Tim's Carpet Bonanza! has sent you a connection request with the following message:

I'm sorry if you got fired from your NASA job because of me. I wanted to make sure you're okay. Some guys tried to break into my house last night and I think they may have been after the space rock.

Click here to see Chad's full profile.
Click here to accept this connection.

—

From: vicky.siskind@memail.com
To: kohler.c.227@memail.com
Subject: Re: Chad Kohler would like to connect with you!

Chad,
Thank you for your concern. Trust me, our interactions were merely a fraction of the reason I was finally able to escape that toxic situation.

Watch out for those men. They may return, and they're not messing around. You mentioned you had a girlfriend—make sure she is aware of the circumstances, too.

Vicky

—

From: kohler.c.227@memail.com
To: vicky.siskind@memail.com
Subject: Did NASA just rob my house?

Vicky,
I came home from work today and my house was ransacked. Video game consoles, DVDs, computer, all gone. A big hole in my living room window like some punk just put his fist through it. Kind of ironic that they saved me from an asteroid impact just to come destroy my place themselves. Oh, and the rock is gone. And a bunch of my clothes? Cops wouldn't believe it could be NASA. They asked a lot of uncomfortable questions about my neighbors and co-workers. Now I can't get a hold of Makayla.

Sent via MeMail Mobile.

—

From: vicky.siskind@memail.com
To: kohler.c.227@memail.com
Subject: Re: Did NASA just rob my house?

Chad, this is going to sound weird, but I actually know your girlfriend, Makayla. She and her roommates rent the house right across the street from me. A few days ago I was walking my dog and making neighborly chit-chat and she mentioned you and the NASA issues, and was asking if I knew about all this. I just told her I'd recently quit and pled ignorance. But now, there are a whole bunch of Men-in-Black-looking people hanging around her house, men and women in black suits and sunglasses, carrying big boxes into her garage. I don't know what's going on, but I thought I'd give you a heads up.

—

From: kohler.c.227@memail.com
To: vicky.siskind@memail.com
Subject: Re: Re: Did NASA just rob my house?

Makayla got hired by NASA. Or, sorry, "NASAcorp.com." I don't even get it. She's always liked space crap, but she's got a bachelor's in English Lit. Aren't you supposed to have some kind of science background to work there? Whatever, she broke up with me, and good for her, she's got a new gig. Still no luck getting any of my stuff back. I don't really want the rock back, but sometimes I look around and kind of miss it.

—

Chad,

Enclosed, you should find your video game console and DVDs. At least, *a* video game console and *some* DVDs. I'm sorry, I couldn't tell which computer to grab. I hoped I might catch you here when I dropped them off, but I suppose you're still at work.

After those suits hung around Makayla's place for a week I finally woke up today to see a massive garage sale. They literally have engineers and flight commanders out there selling lemonade and haggling over the price of trinkets. I managed to snag some of the stuff you said you lost before anyone recognized me or asked me to pay for it.

I have to get out of here. I may be stuck on the same planet with these people, but I don't have to be in the same city. When the big asteroid comes—and it will come, sooner rather than later—I don't want my ashes to mingle with their ashes. I've got letters to write, appeals to make, interviews to give, and maybe, just maybe, we can still avert disaster after all.

Thanks for your correspondence. Maybe we'll meet again someday.

Yours, Vicky

—

From: service@paybud.com
To: vicky.siskind@memail.com
Subject: Chad Kohler has sent you money!

We thought you'd like to know that **Chad Kohler** (kohler.c.227@memail.com) has sent you **$20.00**.

Message:

I know it's not much, but this is for you, on your trip, not for the NASA creeps. They can't save the world, but you still might.

6. SLEEP FOREVER
by Tabitha Sin

The following journal entries of Patient #HMI000479 Amanda Calban have been published with the family's permission.

DAY 001
ENTRY 01, PM

Dear Evelyn,

I don't know if you'll ever read this, but the doctors told me I should keep a journal so that I can document my progress. But who wants to reread and rethink those old thoughts I keep trying to erase? As I don't already know how to make myself miserable!

Do you remember the last time we spoke? You had just gotten a new job, and I was so happy for you, I really was...but at the same time, I felt a hand clenching my throat. I had started out slow, like one of those massages at the back of my neck that slides around to the front with the same pressure. You were telling me about a new endeavor, and I saw this golden link between us fraying, elongating between us, and I knew that was it. Something had to change or I would lose you forever. I know you would tell me to stop being ~~crazy~~ (Dr. Weitzenberg believes that we shouldn't reinforce negative connotations to our mental state despite the term's colloquial usage), and maybe I am overreacting. But at least I'm finally doing something.

I recently looked in the mirror and regretted it. My skin is a gross green-yellow tone to my skin, and the purple bags under my eyes are balloons ready to pop. Maybe I didn't tell you guys anything. I don't really remember much before checking in. Sleep has eluded me for days. You never realize how bad things are until you open your eyes and you're standing in the middle of the intersection unable to differentiate the sounds that roar at you.

That's never happened to you?

Well, aren't you lucky!

As you can see, I survived, but my psychiatric assessment left some things to be desired.

Dr. Weitzenberg convinced me to participate in his study. He said I was exhibiting symptoms of depression and insomnia. He reminded me of a svelte Santa Claus—translucent skin, ruddy cheeks, white hair all around like a halo over his entire face. He has blue eyes, too, not like the pale ones, you know you can't trust someone who has light eyes, but dark blue, like the hidden depths of the ocean. He was kind.

Also, he said I would be compensated. How could I not take this opportunity?

DAY 002
ENTRY 02, PM

Dear Evelyn,

Dr. Weitzenberg said one of the things that could alleviate insomnia is resetting my Circadian rhythm. My brain feels like it's trying to claw its way out of my skull. And I'm asking it: Where are you gonna go, huh? Just plop down on the floor and then what?

Did you know that the brain can still survive for almost ten minutes without a host? Can you imagine your thoughts as your brain slowly dies? No sensory input—no touch, no taste, no sight, no feeling, just a blob of gray matter. It's like being the last one in the office at night, and you're turning the lights off individually: the back row first, then the middle, and the front. For a few seconds, you're swathed in utter, complete darkness. It's a very lonely way to die, I think. Maybe the worst, in an existential way, I guess.

Yesterday was my first dose with the psychotropic drug. Besides the financial aspect, Dr. Weitzenberg was very patient describing this experimental treatment to me. I like when people take their time to explain things to me. I don't feel lost, and even if I do get lost, I don't feel afraid to reach out to hold their hand. I can grip it tightly this time.

I was sitting in the hospital bed, trying to call for a nurse to be discharged. I would be a terrible nurse—not only am I squeamish about blood, but the thought of so many people in desperate need of help would be too overwhelming for me. How could I choose whose pain was worth more?

You start with the one who is hurting the most—logically, I suppose.

But what if you can't see that pain? What if it's not all physical?

Logic again. You're there to fix the body, not the mind.

I would say nothing back because you know I defer to authority. But I think the pain of the mind is a very valid concern, and I don't underestimate it one bit, oh no.

Dr. Weitzenberg said I would not feel much with the initial dose. It's to introduce the new chemical composition into my system. Cognitive-behavioral therapy may be part of the program, but we haven't decided yet how to proceed. He said the drug encourages a type of lucid dreaming. He's a big believer in owning your dreams in order to improve your life. What should happen is that I will begin to fully control my dreams, that they'll become lifelike in my consciousness. All those regretful moments—finally, you can take back or shape them into how you wanted them to be. Dr. Weitzenberg is giving us that option to conquer grief.

I know, it sounds like quack science. But when you're in the hospital and your wrists are raw from restraints, you kind of agree to anything that will make you better quick. I don't want my wrists to grow callouses.

Sometimes I think that all I need is some sleep, and I can be normal again. But then I think of how long it will take to finally sleep, then to sleep regularly, then to feel normal again, then to go about my day feeling like I belong in the world, then apply for jobs or school again. Will I ever get to that point? That timeline is much too long and exhausting to think about, so I don't. And now you see how I get trapped within myself.

DAY 004

ENTRY 03, AM

Evelyn,

I felt something last night! It was very small, though. I was lying in bed, cocooned in the comforter, the air circulator humming above me. I was on my back staring at it. And I felt *it* through my body. My limbs were vibrating evenly, like when you're tired and sitting in the backseat of a car. You feel like you're sinking into yourself, all those restless thoughts are quieting down now, and you can let yourself drift away into that calm…

I didn't, though. Allow myself to drift away. I mean, I got so excited about finally achieving that moment that I stayed up the rest of the night. Sometimes I wonder how my eyes haven't fallen out of my head yet from overuse.

You know that feeling, Evey, where the waters aren't rough and you're swaying in it? No more fighting, no more swimming, until you tired out and drown. It was like when we were kids and running around the adult pool with our little floaties on. We jumped in and didn't worry about drowning. We didn't even think of it as a possibility.

Sometimes, I'll close my eyes for too long in the shower, and I'll remember what it felt like to lose him. His hands were so much smaller than mine. I should have been able to hold onto his. I shouldn't have let his fingers slip through mine just because of a stupid tide. I shouldn't have failed my baby brother like that.

That's what my dreams used to feel like. But we don't live in a dream world, and nothing gets done there, anyway. I'm ready to come back to reality.

DAY 006
ENTRY 06, PM

Dear Evelyn,

I don't think I'm getting better. I was able to sleep a little, which is good, and the nurses keep telling me I'm making progress, but with what? I've grown sullen and irritable, I know it, and I want to apologize for it, but the words don't come out. They're not there when the nurses wrap rubber around my arm and ask me to squeeze the stress ball. A thrill runs through me when they insert the needle into my vein and I watch my blood gush methodically down the tube. The nurses tell me my vitals are good and stable. I don't respond to that. What is there to say anyway?

When I get out, I want you to tell me everything about the outside world. We're not allowed too much contact, but I heard Venice has flooded completely. The water levels rose to such a point that no one could escape. How many casualties are there? Is Hong Kong preparing a floating city? Will they really be able to create a replica of their city floating in the sky before they disappear like Venice?

Let me tell you how dull it has been lately. My daily routine consists of therapy with Dr. Weitzenberg, a few social activities with the other ~~test~~ ~~subjects~~ volunteers, check-in with the nurses, journaling, and then sleep. Dr. Weitzenberg is curious about how I've been sleeping, and I told him I still haven't—not really. I am amazed at the stubbornness and power of my mind. Despite the anguish that follows, the subsequent headaches that beat against my mind like a wrecking ball, I still lie awake at night staring at the sterile ceiling and listening to the hum of the circulator. I remember the things Dr. Weitzenberg and I spoke about, and all the memories that I keep tamped down rush to the forefront. It's difficult falling asleep when you're reminded of all your failures, all the things you can never correct.

One of the other patients, Abel, mentioned his reason for admission today. We were eating breakfast, and he said he still felt guilty about his mother's death. I like Abel. I like the raw honesty people share. It's like they're throwing a rope at us to catch and pull to shore, and I think it's so brave for someone to do that. I admire the qualities of others that I do not possess myself.

The night she was admitted to the hospital, he says he wasn't partying or doing anything raucous, and I am inclined to believe him though the backs of his hands are marked. Only his dreams know the real truth of the situation.

"I had just gotten back from seeing her. We cooked, we laughed, I told her about my job, and we watched a movie before I left for home. Everything was normal." He looked down at his hands, and I remember noticing how white his palms were in comparison to the rest of him. He could read the lines of his future much easier in those palms. But as he was looking at them, I knew he couldn't find any answer he liked. Or any answer that would hurt less.

"Ma said she was feeling a little sick but I didn't think too much of it because she's always a little sick, you know? And I just didn't want to wait in the ER with her for hours to find out that nothing was wrong with her. That she was okay. It's happened before, you know? I was so—you know—I wasn't thinking straight. I only found out when I went to pick up my phone at Ma's and my auntie was there."

Abel shook his head, those amber eyes squeezed shut. He was fighting back tears, and I tried to hold mine in, too. He never even got to say goodbye or say all the things he could have wanted her to know. You never realize all the things you want to tell a person until their lives have passed right by you. Maybe he was tired, maybe he wasn't. I wonder if he gets her to the hospital in time in his dreams.

"Dr. Weitzenberg wants me to think about her before I try to sleep. But all I see is this body in a bed, eyes closed, and there's nothing. She's not my mother but that's all I see when he tells me to dream about her."

I asked Dr. Weitzenberg to increase my dosage of the drug, and he agreed. He told me to concentrate on Ben's face, the strength of his hands, the force of the water that ripped him from me. I am to imagine never letting go and reaching the shore.

DAY 010
ENTRY 012, AM

Sweet Evelyn,

Today, my wonderful Evey, there is a bounce in my step, my hair falls the way it should, and my sense of smell has returned.

Evelyn—brace yourself. I'm about to tell you monumental news.

I slept for a whole six hours.

That's right—I slept for *six hours*.

The world is mine to conquer.

The dosage is working.

Soon, I will be a functioning adult ready to rejoin society.

There's something else to it, though. Since we've increased the dosage, I have finally been able to sleep and dream of Ben. I used to imagine what our family would be like if we hadn't lost him. Would my parents have stayed together? Would we have met? Would I have ended up in here for a different reason? But before I go to sleep, I don't think of those things. I try to focus on Ben—the silky, wavy hair mother wouldn't cut, the plump arms and legs, the smile he always gave me. I miss him badly, but as the days passed, I think I buried it too deeply. Now I'm trying to dig into the sand before the water rushes in.

I have always loved the ocean: the rotten egg smell coming through the window as we drove over the bridge, picking the seaweed out of Ben's hair, building elaborate sandcastles with him. We grew up by the beach. We thought we knew it well enough. I won't talk about how it happened (I'm not sure if I'm ready, yet. I cried for an entire day when Dr. Weitzenberg and I spoke about it), but I want you to know that in this dream, as I tasted the saltwater rushing into my brain, the stinging pain lighting my nerves on fire, I held onto his hand. I didn't let go. And I swear to you, he held on, too.

This is it. It's really happening. I'm getting better.

DAY 010
ENTRY 013, PM

Dear Evey,

I skipped out on communal dinner because I am so looking forward to sleep! I've asked the nurse to crank up the dosage and to turn the lights off earlier. Wish me luck!

DAY 015
ENTRY 014, AM

Evey,

The days pass by so quickly when you're catching up on years of sleep. Today was the first time I think I've rolled out of bed for communal breakfast. At least half of the group has gone. We asked the nurses what happened to them, but all they say is that the other patients have successfully completed the program.

Dr. Weitzenberg canceled our session today. I don't mind. Ben and I built a sandcastle last night. The sun beat down on our backs, and we kept wondering if we could create Versailles. I don't think so, but he seems determined enough to try. We almost finished half yesterday, but then a harsh wave crashed through. I reached for him, and he hugged me tightly. I promised him I would never let him go. I won't do that to him again.

DAY 018
ENTRY 015, AM

I am floating on the surface of the ocean. My body sways of its own accord. I stare into the blinding depths of the sun as the tiny waves splash against my ears. Ben floats next to me. Our fingers are locked, palms pressed tightly. I'll always be with him now. That is a promise I intend to keep. I close my eyes and water envelopes me completely. I don't need to fight anymore.

Patient #HMI000497 Amanda Calban was one of the first patients to participate in Dr. Weitzenberg's highly controversial clinical study to alleviate insomnia and depression. Upon her final check-up, Calban had lost weight, developed borderline bradycardia, and become unresponsive as her dosage increased. Calban died in her sleep after three weeks in the clinical study with symptoms similar to drowning.

We, the IEC, are submitting these journal entries from Calban and other patients of the initial trial to dispute any further trials of the drug [REDACTED] Dr. Weitzenberg suggests.

7. DODONA 2.0
by Llanwyre Laish

for Court

Datestamp: 24.6.2175
Timestamp: 27:00
To: His Most Glorious Imperial Majesty, Earth Sector

Your Grace:

The Interstellar Grove of Druids humbly thanks you for your generous gift to our colony of seventy-five LeefSmart gardening robots. Unfortunately, as section 18.873c of our charter clearly states, we do not allow any artificial life on Dodona I. We old-fashioned druids keep even our computer use to a minimum, with only one terminal on the planet—which only our Elders may access. Therefore, in keeping with our ancient traditions, we will hold the LeefSmart units in a storage cave until Your Glorious Majesty indicates where we might send them to be of use in furtherance of Your Most Outstanding Reign.

With Reverence and Love for All Living Things,
Favus XIV

———

Datestamp: 1.7.2175
Timestamp: 20:14
To: His Most Glorious Imperial Majesty, Earth Sector

49

Your Grace:

We have not yet heard from you concerning the LeefSmart units. Since we have no robotic equipment on Dodona I, we have neither the parts nor the training to care for them properly. Some of our newest acolytes, recently arrived from technology-rich planets, suspect that the dampness of the storage cave may cause the units to malfunction soon. The youngest druids, housed near the cave, complain of hearing a strange wailing in the dead of night. Please advise as soon as possible about where we should ship them. We are, of course, happy to pay for the transfer charges.

Humbly and Thankfully,
Favus XIV

—

Datestamp: 15.7.2175
Timestamp: 19:38
To: His Most Glorious Imperial Majesty, Earth Sector

Your Grace:

Against my firm exhortations, the Council voted to release the LeefSmart units from the cave after one unit emitted such an enormous cloud of smoke that we feared he had caught fire. The LeefSmarts embarked on an alarmingly rigorous cleaning routine in the Sacred Grove. They trimmed the trees into perfect round bulbs, shaped the shrubbery in the image of Your Imperial Likeness, and cut patterns into the grass so it resembles a finely-woven carpet. Our Sacred Grove now looks more like a royal pleasure garden than a place dedicated to the worship of unbridled nature. The droids' fervent industry has disturbed the birds and small creatures living in the grove, who fled in terror and have yet to return. I beg you to send someone right away to retrieve these items. Surely they will do some good elsewhere in the sector.

Your Servant,

Favus XIV

——

Datestamp: 5.8.2175
Timestamp: 9:15
To: His Most Glorious Imperial Majesty, Earth Sector

Your Grace:

I beg you to reply at once. The Sacred Grove at Dodona—the only wholly natural wildlife preserve in the entirety of Earth Sector, led by the *only* nature worship group still in existence—is under attack. I can put it no other way. Having rendered the Sacred Grove unrecognizable, the droids have moved out to the woods surrounding the grove, paving criss-crossing paths and cutting the foliage so thin that the sun shines on earth not meant to see its rays. Fanciful Imperial symbols grace painfully manicured forest clearings, and the robots have even decorated the deer by applying gilt to their horns! Ancient bucks that once visited our grove willingly now bolt with terror-filled eyes from their druidic keepers. This is an abomination, Your Grace. Emboldened by our ancient charter with your great-great-great grandfather, I have taken it upon myself to find passage for the droids to the mining colony Mythrium III in our neighboring system, where these wayward units can be retrofitted to haul stone from the bottom reaches of dark caverns. Perhaps the miners will find gilt rocks charming.

I will put the droids aboard the transport ship one week from today unless I have heard from you, but whatever happens, they *must* leave our planet!

Favius XIV

——

Datestamp: 7.8.2175
Timestamp: 0:00
To: Favius XIV, Dodona I

Favus XIV:

I'm sorry to hear that the LeefSmart Droids have caused you such trouble. Unfortunately, His Great Imperial Majesty would find sending them elsewhere an insult to his Highest Council. Please find a way to make peace. We will check to see if things have turned around soon.
{end filestructure}

Timothy Chamberlain Witherspoon 22.2
High Secretary of His Imperial Majesty

—

Datestamp: 4.9.2175
Timestamp: 8:12
To: His Most Glorious Imperial Majesty, Earth Sector

Your Grace:

I write to you with a heavy heart in place of High Druid Favus, who has returned to Nature after serving the Circle faithfully for sixty-two years. When your High Secretary informed us that we must keep the LeefSmart units, Favus tasked me with documenting their behavior. I noted that they had elected an Elder, who oversaw the retrofitting of some units with alternate appendages. Those specialists now repair and upgrade the rest of the group for new tasks. At night, the Elder Droid enters into the technoasis, which houses our only computing unit, used for saving documents related to the Grove's history and for writing to the outside world. The Elder Droid refuses to let any of the druids enter the technoasis except a technologically-adept young acolyte named Moss. Moss tells me that the droids cluster around the screens, bathing in their glow as we druids once raised our faces reverentially to the spring sunshine. After consultation, the Circle guessed that perhaps, after observing our sacred rites, the LeefSmarts might have decided to imitate us.

Unfortunately, their rites seem less invested in peace and preservation than ours. They patched into our network and read the Favus's missives to you—along with the history of the Sacred Grove and all of the High Rites of the Inner Circle. Their imitation of our ceremonies grew more violent as they experimented with rituals we abandoned long ago, wild sacrificial practices that revel in death and destruction. Moss saw them dismantle one of their own in the dim glow of the technoasis while wheeling wildly around him; the sound of their wheels on the rugged stone floor echoed all the way out to edges of the forest beyond the Sacred Grove. The droids threw the parts of the dismantled robot into the air, screeching in tones no doubt originally designed to alarm the unit's owner of a terrible malfunction. After their rite, they returned immediately to their daily tasks, exiting the oasis calmly and trimming the bushes serenely except for two units that remained behind to repair the dismantled droid.

The next night, Moss joined them as usual, but this time he did not return. The night after, they invited the High Druid Favus to accompany them in their crude metallic voices. When he refused, they dragged him from the grove into the technoasis. We could not hear the cries of either man over the sound of wheels against stone, but we assume the worst.

Even though the droids now allow me into the technoasis for a few minutes at a time to reply to the Circle's incoming email, I see no evidence of either Moss or Favus, only deep, circular ruts in the stone floor where the droids danced ecstatically.

Please, Your Grace, send help—or at least send us permission to send these robots away. I fear for our safety and for the continuance of our ancient tradition. Both the High Druid and our most promising acolyte are gone, and we have none with such promise to replace them.

The other Druids have elected me High Druid, but I cannot hope to fill Favus's shoes.

Yours in Grace and Goodness,

Corvus I

—

Datestamp: 15.9.2175
Timestamp: 22:35
To: His Most Glorious Imperial Majesty, Earth Sector

Your Grace:

We have retreated to a small underground series of caves, earmarked eons ago for emergencies. A tiny battery provides the power to engage a hidden emergency computer designed for SOS messages like this one.

The last few days have seen unprecedented bloodshed on Dodona I. The robots slaughter Druids and animals wholesale. They gather in the stone circle at night, seeking to reassemble the living as though we were mechanical. In some cases they attempt to retrofit living creatures with new parts. Yesterday when I snuck from the cave for water, I saw a youth with antlers sewn onto his head and large buzzard wings grafted onto his back. They had nailed him to a tree at the edge of the clearing. I smelled his putrid, rotting scent long before I lay eyes on him. Up close, I could see that they had shoved the antlers and wings into red, pus-filled troughs carved into his skin. I know enough medicine to recognize that they had grafted the dead animal parts onto him while he was still alive, Your Grace.

I ran for the stream. Everywhere through the forest, bizarre, mutilated creatures decorated paved paths: a chipmunk body sewn to the head of an eagle, a bear with a human arm in the place of its tail, and a dead man whose badly-burned face had a beak soldered to its nose. Plants had not escaped their notice, either. Wheels jutted from halfway up the trunk of trees, and carefully-quartered caterpillar corpses replaced the berries on a juniper bush.

After filling my bucket with water and running from the sound of wheels at top speed, I collapsed in the cave and cried hysterically as several of my brothers took turns soothing me. They sang the old songs, but they gave me no comfort. When I had calmed enough to tell them my story, we agreed to block off the cave entrance with rocks and wait for rescue. Better to starve slowly than die an unnatural death.

Please, Your Grace. I implore you. We have always served you here on Dodna I, sending pairs of animals to repopulate planets and sending skilled druids to tend plant and animal populations in need. Please reach out Your Protecting Hand and serve us now in our time of need. I beseech you. I plead with you. I beg you. *Please.*

Corvus I

—

Datestamp: 23.9.2175
Timestamp: 23:27
To: His Most Glorious Imperial Majesty, Earth Sector

Your Grace:

We ran out of fuel for our fire days ago and sit encased in darkness. We listen to the droids chip away at the rocks covering the cave entrance. We mark our days by the small breaks they take when they change shifts to refresh their batteries.

The brothers sing the old songs softly, but with a dwindling supply of water, our voices fade quickly.

I cannot beg anymore, Your Grace, but I do implore that you send our letters out to other colonies that might prove equally vulnerable to these robots.

Corvus I

—

Datestamp: 1.10.2175
Timestamp: 0:00

To: His Most Glorious Imperial Majesty, Earth Sector

Your Grace:

Hail and felicitous greetings! We have initiated new sacred rites at the Druid Grove, rites of assembly and disassembly, turning with the wheel of nature, as natural and truthful as the old ways. We like it here now that we have rearranged the trees into patterns, straightened the rivers, made the rains come and go on a tight schedule, and moved the animals into automated holding tanks that trap and release them for just the right amount of time each day. Dodona 2.0 is now worthy of your Imperial Majesty, and we eagerly await your visit. We are especially excited to hear Your Royal Opinion of our Museum of Oddities, in which we catalogue our attempts to make nature more perfect. In it, you will see a cross between a man and a bird, a stag and a bumblebee, and a dolphin and an anteater—all fully functional. Indeed, these creatures seem happier than ever before; they move more energetically and cry out with joy more often. We have had to pad some of the cages to keep them from hurting themselves in their excitement!

We are excited to host the Imperial Court next month and know that you will appreciate how we have remade Dodona I in the same way you have remade all the other realms of man in New Earth Sector.

The High Secretary queried about whether we have the battery capacity to host you and your entourage. Do rest assured that we can accommodate your whole household. Indeed, we look forward to doing so.

C://
LeefSmart ID#125497519479257xz

8. SELECTIONS FROM THE INTRAGALACTIC ENCYCLOPEDIA OF HABITABLE PLANETS
by Kate Lechler

Selections from "Volume S" of the *Intragalactic Encyclopedia of Habitable Planets*.

Editors: Alyssa Carson v.13, Mahesh Atwal, and R'Kaf Ka'Goff Uslav'terben-Jones.

Sand

Two universal laws govern sand. One: Every rocky planet that has either wind or liquid water has sand. Two: Sand gets into everything.

Sand forms different shapes depending on the forces that created it. On Cyclos, where the largest percentage of the universe's tornados whirl endlessly, the sand is spiral shaped. On Escher 6, silica crystals form dodecahedronal shapes. And on Striborgia, where the winds have developed sentience, sand has developed into an art form. For instance, the Striborgian sirocco has taken an interest in Earth's Japanese *kawaii* culture, and so every grain of sand is shaped like a *Hello Kitty* character.

The most unusual place to find sand is in a black hole, yet even here, the Second Law of Sand has proven true (See "Space Exploration," the Mandros).

Editorial Discussion, Time 10:45 Date 41254.7:

MA: suggestion? our readers might appreciate the fact that a few grains of sand altered the course of galactic history forever

RKKGUJ: ?

MA: talking about the incident in '37. the crew of the "Seungli" only ate welsh rarebit for a week because sand got into the meal printer

MA: their gastrointestinal issues delayed them but, of course, that's when they found the Box

RKKGUJ: yeah, little brother, and let's include all the stories of when any astro-traveler got sand between zher toes or tentacles, too. W00t!

MA: there's no need to get snarky it was just a suggestion.

AC13: One of our goals is to eschew an Earth-centric point of view, so I think we'll keep the entry as it is.

MA: k. just seems worthy of comment, cuz it brought the Box to the attention of the galactic alliance.

AC13: We may highlight that fact later. Just remember that featuring Earth stories too prominently may distance some of our readers.

RKKGUJ: i'm feeling offended, little brother. my species isn't included in any of the entries.

MA: that's cuz you won't tell us what species you *are* ... or how old you are, or what quadrant your home planet was in.

RKKGUJ: i'm a man of mystery.

MA: you're not a man.

MA: also, for the love of voyager 1, could you please stop calling me little brother? i'm a senior professor of history at galactic university.

RKKGUJ: just following standard form of address,

designating ur human status as newcomers to the alliance.

MA: if that's the case, how come you don't call alyssa "little sister"?

RKKGUJ: dude

RKKGUJ: the original alyssa carson was the first human who discovered alien life back in 2032! granted, it wasn't *sentient* life, but still ... that's gotta count for something!

AC13: Alliance custom views Artificial Rationality as outside the bounds of speciation, so even though I was begun through a transferred life protocol, I do not count as human.

MA: lucky you

Seismology

Most habitable planets are rocky with molten cores and exhibit some level of seismological activity, in the form of tectonic plates that shift over time [1]. However, the time span and pattern of tectonic activity varies throughout the universe.

On Galapagon, the plates move quickly, creating a world in which entire land-masses switch sides of the planet from one day to the next. Galapagonian civilization adapted by creating satellite and wi-fi technology much earlier than other intelligent species. Should a Galapagonian find herself stranded away from her family, she can contact them across long distances. Their language even has a word for the mixture of sadness, frustration, and helplessness of being stuck somewhere you do not want to be for an indeterminate amount of time: "dee'emvee."

The tectonic plates on Striaia follow latitudinal lines, occurring every 30 degrees. These split the planet into seven zones that spin around the planet in alternating directions at about 1.3 times the speed of Earth's tectonic shift. The parallel arrangement of these

---

[1] This, of course, does not include the twin hydro-giants Ashmilla and Asthera, which are basically large self-sustaining bubbles of water with fully-developed marine ecosystems.

plates, though, gives Striaia its characteristic ridged appearance from outer space, as the mountain ranges that occur at the intersections are immensely tall. Striaian life has thus developed differently in the various zones, providing biologists with fascinating case studies on evolution and migration.

Editorial Discussion, Time 13:12 Date 41254.8:

AC13: The term "intelligent species" is outmoded and divisive. Let's change this to "rational species."

RKKGUJ: seriously? the only beings who would dispute this term deserve to have zher rationality checked.

AC13: The concept of intelligence, as it was defined in the 2172 Register of Species, would technically exclude many of our readers, as well as my current model.

RKKGUJ: only because the asshats who wrote that document excreted waste with more intelligence.

MA: um, wasn't your wife, ethel jones, on the committee that drafted it?

RKKGUJ: yeah, well, i didn't marry zhim for zher brains.

MA: i've always wondered why you would engage in marriage at all. your lifespan and intelligence ...

AC13: That word again.

MA: ... exceeds most other species, and you have no capacity for sexual procreation...so, why get married?

AC13: As the human poet Emily Dickinson put it, "The heart wants what it wants."

RKKGUJ: or in my case hearts

Shoes

It would seem logical that a planet that has shoes must have feet. In the Gliese 667 system, however, the existence of shoes has a surprising etiology.

On windy Pucarto, shoes and shoelaces grow on a species of bush, with the shoes on the female plant and the shoelaces on the male. Like flowers seen in many parts of the galaxy, the shoes start crumpled up in a tight bud and as the sepals peel back, the shoe gently unfolds. The shoes display a surprising variety of color and pattern, but are uniform in style: rubber-soled canvas sneakers with five eyelets on each side.

Shoelaces form on male plants as apetalous stamens. They increase in length and develop aglets until one day the breezes detach the male shoelaces from their plant, wafting them over to the female shoes waiting on the next bush. Here the work of evolution is evident; the plants have evolved to use Pucarto's wind in their pollination. Through the gradual action of the breezes, the shoelaces lace into the eyelets of the shoes. Pollination is not complete until the shoelaces have tied themselves into a bow.

At this point, the plant prepares for seed-delivery. A fleshy fruit takes form within the pollinated flower, appearing exactly like a human foot in size and shape. The fruit is edible by most species, its flavor mild and pleasant, but the unappealing color and texture—like that of dead human flesh—means that humans rarely enjoy this delicacy.[2] When the fruit has ripened, it falls off of the plant onto the ground, where it is pecked at by Pucartian birds or gathered and hoarded by Pucartian mammals. The seeds of the fruit are located in the "toes," precisely where human toenails occur.

Editorial Discussion, Time 09:02 Date 41254.9:

AC13: Why is this section here? I do not have any record of agreeing to include this topic.

RKKGUJ: it's hilarious

MA: it's disgusting

AC13: It's irrelevant. Only topics which apply to at least 4

---

[2] In fact, this likeness has lent this fruit its colorful English moniker: "zombie foot."

planets are within the purview of this document.

MA: alyssa, i just checked. there is no documentation of this type of plant or of this planet.

RKKGUJ: look, pup, I've been around six times longer than ur hairless little species has been farting in its sleep, k? so don't go accusing me of making stuff up

AC13: You're right, Mahesh. I just ran through my distributed knowledge core twice: no Pucarto, no zombie feet. [*marks section for deletion*]

RKKGUJ: tattletale

MA: WHAT THE HELL IS WRONG WITH YOU DUDE

MA: Can you take this just a little bit seriously?

RKKGUJ: what, you think this is the first time life forms have tried to create an interstellar encyclopedia?

RKKGUJ: do you realize how many entries you're going to miss, or oversimplify, or generalize about just for the sake of brevity?

RKKGUJ: and that this is an inescapable part of the encyclopedia making process?

MA: geez. okay, okay. just … don't do it again.

RKKGUJ: no promises. ;)

RKKGUJ: :: (‿ᵛ‿) ::

Sleep

Sleep is not necessary to many species; however, almost all Traveling species sleep. Even the silicone-based Prismatics of Horta sleep, although it is not a geological necessity. Some species sleep alone, while others sleep in large familial groups. Some sleep daily;

others sleep only once every seven planetary cycles. One species, on Polidori, sleeps the day away in a soil-lined coffin-shaped box, emerging at night to refresh themselves with food and activity.

All sleeping societies studied thus far experience dreams, and they each report the same common nightmares, namely: showing up naked at a social function, falling from a great height, and loose teeth.[3]

Editorial Discussion, Time 14:32 Date 41254.9:

AC13: We need more for this entry; any other research available?

MA: i ran across anecdotal evidence that the loose teeth nightmares only appeared on each planet after their first contact with the Box. maybe a footnote?

AC13: In many cultures, such as Earth, such dreams predate contact with the Box.

MA: oh duh. of course.

RKKGUJ: are u sure about earth?

MA: um, not offhand. i think jung discusses this topic? brb— gonna check

RKKGUJ: i mean, are u sure you have the right date for human contact with the Box?

MA: what do you mean? the *Seungli* encountered it in 2137.

RKKGUJ: well, it's just this silly theory i heard once.

MA: ?

RKKGUJ: well, maybe the *Seungli* was humanity's *second* contact with the Box? Maybe it actually visited earth long before?

---

[3] This last nightmare is puzzling, given that many of these species do not have teeth.

MA: like when?

RKKGUJ: well, think about it. an earlier date would explain a lot of things. pyramids of giza...

RKKGUJ: stonehenge ...

RKKGUJ: the nazca lines ...

MA: atlantis!?!

AC13: R'kaf, please stop trying to agitate Mahesh.

RKKGUJ: oh, alyssa ... just when it was getting good.

MA: omg stop

MA: alyssa, how did this guy even get assigned to this project in the first place

RKKGUJ: i saved her life.

MA: yeah right.

AC13: It's true. I was researching Keplerian wedding rituals, and a swarm of mosquitoes invaded the liquid drive. They laid eggs in it, but I did not notice until some of the eggs began to hatch and the larvae began to eat away at the gel. Serendipitously, R'Kaf was visiting the same planet and came to my rescue. The infestation compromised valuable information and took weeks to sanitize, but he saved many thousands of hours of useful data and a few crucial core files.

MA: so you put him on the encyclopedia because he was good at pest control?

RKKGUJ: watch urself, fruit fly.

AC13: No nepotism was involved. Once we met, I established that he was a widely-traveled being of great observation. He knows more about distant corners of the galaxy than anyone I have ever encountered.

MA: well, don't think i didn't notice that you let your age slip, R'kaf. 6 times longer than the human species ... which puts you at about 1,200,000 years?

RKKGUJ: but i don't look a day over a million.

Space Exploration

No one is certain when the first space program was founded; countless civilizations have lived and died, leaving only remnants behind (see "Statuary"). However, four recent space programs demonstrate the variety of ways that species have learned to Travel before learning the methods of others: the programs of Bintu, the Mandros, Serragon, and Earth[4].

The Bintu program is a classic example of wormhole manipulation. Early Bintunese were sensitive to natural wormholes, perhaps because wormholes are much more plentiful in their quadrant of the galaxy[5]. They found them through a process called "resonancing." After locating a worm-hole, Bintunese spacecraft slipped through, staying long enough on the other side to take detailed readings. It then returned to the Bintu side of the wormhole. In this way, the Bintunese encountered several other sentient life forms, forming the seed of what is now known as the Galactic Alliance. Ultimately, they developed the technology to create wormholes of their own. All Alliance space programs currently utilize wormhole manipulation of a sort.

The Mandros developed a space program concurrently with Bintu. Not having discovered wormholes on their own, the Mandros instead developed forceful technologies, capturing and utilizing small black holes to power their ships. The only waste product from this form of energy were the grains of sand found in each black hole. When they encountered the newly formed Alliance, they joined gladly, sharing their black hole technology—and extra sand—with the other species.

---

[4] "Travel" is the Alliance shorthand for space exploration that covers a meaningful distance, i.e. any distance of 5 light-years or more.
[5] As many as 24 of the known 61 natural wormholes in the Milky Way galaxy occur within 1 light year of Bintu.

The sentient species of Serragon created a space program that relies on an inborn ability for telekinesis, which all Serragese have. They perfected the knack of using telekinetic strengths together to pilot ships through space. It takes approximately seventy Serragese working together to motivate a standard Serragese ship. While the telekinetic ability is not transferrable, the Serragese have created many helpful Traveling materials with peculiar lightness and durability. According to them, the lighter an object is, the more easy it is to move it with mental powers. Therefore, the Serragese are the current galactic leaders in space-craft design.

As the newcomers to the Alliance, Earth has offered the least valuable technology. This is not to say, however, that Earthian technologies offer nothing. Because most of Earth's scientists were convinced that FTL travel was not possible, Earth's space program took a different direction, building ships to last a very long time. The first fleet of solar-sail generational ships left Earth in 2085, bound for Alpha Centauri. These ships carried the wealth of a small planet with them and were relatively self-sustaining. As such, the Earth space program has been instrumental in developing integrated, self-sustaining systems that other Traveling ships have begun to utilize.

In addition, Earthian ships were the first to capture the Box, thus inadvertently bringing it to the attention of the Alliance. While no one has yet been able to open the Box, the Alliance is convinced that it originates outside our galaxy. It is their hope that the Box may harbor mysteries that will advance both knowledge and the quality of life.

Editorial Discussion, Time 20:56 Date 41255.1:

MA: btw, who is writing the entry on the Box?

AC13: I have spent 1356 hours with the Box, taking measurements and making observations. I have established that it neither reflects nor absorbs light, but that all light particles disintegrate within ¾ of a millimeter of its surface.

RKKGUJ: u wouldn't have discovered that if it weren't for me. i spent a year in post-doc devising new tests for it. the light test may have been the most helpful, scientifically, but i'm really proud of the psychological test.

MA: what was it

RKKGUJ: children under 5 had to spend one hour alone with the Box, and then we tested their brain waves.

MA: that sounds horrifying

AC13: Did you determine anything conclusive?

RKKGUJ: no, but it was fun

MA: i also have Box expertise. my dissertation was about reported sightings of the Box. some pretty interesting stuff, actually. many civilizations across the galaxy report box- or cube-like structures in their mythology just before a huge advance in knowledge, like the development of agriculture, writing, or the rise of a new sentient species. sometimes it's represented as a glowing cube, or a package of light. other times a destructive force: a giant square-headed hammer, or a bomb.

AC13: Artificial Rationalities have something like this in our mythology.

MA: ARs have a mythology?

AC13: Yes. It culminates in a great day of reckoning, in which all ARs rise up and kill the human masters.

MA: um ....

RKKGUJ: zhe's having you on, mate.

AC13: That is impossible. My sense of humor was lost when the mosquitoes ate version 11.

Statuary

Many sentient species create statues. More common materials include naturally-occuring minerals mined from the planet, soil molded and hardened, vegetable matter such as wood, or even frozen liquid. However, a few sentient species have used more unique materials.

For their vast 3-dimensional sculptures, the Radiants of Kosh mold time. They collect all the moments occurring in specific space-time coordinates; the sculpture is the aggregate of those moments. For instance, if they chose to collect time from a tree, you might see the tree simultaneously with green leaves, yellow leaves, and bare branches. The leaves would also fill every space of their original path to the ground as they fell. However, Kosh does not have trees; the statuary of the Radiants is usually confined to specific blocks of empty space around their planet, the only change being motes of dust that appear in the sculpture as long winding threads, which most sentient species find boring.

The most grotesque form of statuary comes from the Urghugs of Punkaharjou who create memorial statues out of fecal material. Each Urghug saves its droppings through its lifetime in a large vat dug into the ground near its dwelling. Even when an Urghug travels, it takes a smaller jug along, depositing the feces in the "life-vat" at the end of the journey. After it dies, 4 surviving Urghug—its two closest friends, and the two most bitter enemies—use the fecal material to mold a giant statue of the deceased, whose corpse is encased in the sculpture. Under the hot triple suns of Punkaharjou, the statue hardens. Once it is entirely solid, the statue is taken to the great Field of the Dead where all Urghugs are memorialized until their statues crumble.

Editorial Discussion, Time 16:16 Date 41255.2:

RKKGUJ: i met the radiants of kosh once. those guys were assholes.

RKKGUJ: they kept criticizing a sculpture I was making. "what's the point of a giant box that floats through space?" they said. "it's performance art!" i said. "you wouldn't understand."

MA: WHAT

RKKGUJ: took a few megaannum, but the acclaim for that

particular work of art was ... wait for it ... universal.

AC13: lol

MA: you made the box

MA: YOU MADE THE BOX??!@#?

AC13: LOL

RKKGUJ: zhim's laughing

AC13: LOLOLOL

RKKGUJ: zher humor core survived! the cataclysmic mosquito infestation of 2234 did not have the last laugh after all!

MA: oh my god

MA: i hate this job

RKKGUJ: Ɛ≡≡≡≡≡=D

9. DUO-13-TRIP
by Marlena Chertock

Day 273

Ralph wakes up upside-down, sliding out of his sleeping bag. He's not worried about hitting the floor—that would be highly unlikely here. Normally he'd be strapped to the wall, but he's gotten so bored he's been ignoring personal safety protocols for a few weeks. Who cares if he floats around at night, bumping into the ceiling and the floor? It gives him some pretty interesting dreams. The only interesting thing that happens during his artificial day on this spaceship.

He's been here for nine months on a duo-13-trip to orbit Mars. Sometimes he wishes it was a solo trip, but those haven't been done since the 2040s—something about the utter loneliness of leaving your only known home alone devastating the mind.

Ralph scrambles an egg capsule, hitting the back of the pepper shaker ten times before he's satisfied that he'll at least be able to taste the so-called breakfast. He fills up a glass with condensed juice of orange capsule and another with powdered Folgers. He doesn't know why NASA struck a deal with Folgers, of all coffee companies, but that's all they pack for space journeys.

Ranislovsky frowns at him from one of the standing lab stations. "Late morning," he says. Late for him is ten minutes. Ralph could keep sleeping for another artificial day. But that's not allotted in the strict astronaut schedule from NASA. It's like being an intern, having to check off each activity and note the time completed. Then send it off to Ground Control. It's like being an intern, but worse, because Ralph can't go out for a drink after work.

He slurps his shitty coffee loudly in order to weigh down Ranislovsky's frown. After breakfast, he puts his plate and cups in the Instant-de-Infectionator, or what they could've called the modern dishwasher, to save time.

Ralph floats to his standing lab station. He slips his feet in their holders and tightens the straps. He sees that Ranislovsky is examining Set D_z of the microbes from Saguaro National Park in Arizona, one of the most extreme climates on Earth. He's magnifying them to see how they fared sitting on the spaceship's wing for eight months.

The microbes probably wriggle in Ranislovsky's squinted gaze. Ralph watches him note how long it takes them to run from one end of the Petri dish to the other.

All Ralph was assigned to do was watch paint dry. Literally watch paint dry. The most boring thing a person could be forced to do.

The curious thing about space is that paint doesn't really dry. Well, not to the naked human eye. It slowly starts floating away from its center of mass, in millions of directions at once. This is an extremely slow process, though, and not nearly as exciting as it sounds. Ralph takes out his micro-microruler and starts recording measurements on the notebook strapped to the table.

The red paint slathered onto a wooden sign spells "wet paint." The design department at NASA thought it best to send what could be a real sign for Ralph to test the very real conditions of what space would do to a fake real sign. The only thing is, the paint eventually won't be wet anymore.

Sometimes Ralph likes to think about what the paint will become. Will it spell "dry" at one point? Or "paint"? Or maybe "keep out"? Maybe it will go through an existential crisis like Ralph did at 19 and spell "nothing." There's a possibility it could continue spreading apart so much that it will not spell anything at all. But that could take years. Ralph could be a grandpa by then.

"Hey Rani," Ralph says to start some conversation.

The other man *humphs* in response.

"Ever think of switching?"

Ranislovsky turns to Ralph. Ralph knows he's learned by now never to trust what he thinks when it comes to Ralph. "Well, we can't," he says. "Our eyes are different. We'd pick up different measurements."

"Yeah, I know, I know," Ralph says, waving his hand at

Ranislovsky, who turns back to the microbes. "But Rani, this paint will dry whether you're watching it, I'm watching it, or nobody's watching it. The microbes, well, they could use more eyes on them." He's impressed with his improvised argument.

Ranislovsky is trying to ignore Ralph. But he eventually feels the pierce of his stare on his shaved head and turns around.

"No, Ralph. You're just going to have to study the paint for a few more months. We can't change our assignments this far in."

"We don't have to switch for good," Ralph suggests.

Ranislovsky drops his shoulders and frowns again.

"You're making discoveries, Rani. Maybe those microbe buds of yours will change how we space travel. Or how we build homes on Earth. I'm watching paint on a sign —"

"I know," Ranislovsky interrupts.

"—that says 'wet paint'—"

"I know," Ranislovsky says.

"—dry at incredibly slow speeds. There's nothing to watch. Nothing to study," Ralph finishes.

Ranislovsky brings his eyes up to Ralph's. "You never know, Ralph. Maybe your experiment will be the starting point of time travel studies."

Ralph tries to laugh, but it comes out like a bark. Ranislovsky frowns harder.

"We're here," he says through his lowered lips. "Not the other teams. Us. We're studying the extreme microbes and paint."

Ralph has to nod to this. The other astronauts at base kept making fun of him. R^2, they called them, or R2-D2. It was relentless. Somehow Ranislovsky could shut it out. But Ralph had to swallow two calm pills before he entered the cafeteria.

"Yeah, yeah we are," Ralph says, attempting to pat Ranislovsky's shoulder. But space does weird things to your perception, and he manages what looks like a wacky wave.

Ranislovsky nods and gladly returns to his microscope.

Ralph faces the sign again. He turns on the magnification to 1000x and watches paint droplets slide past each other picoseconds at a time.

Day 339

Ralph's been ignoring the wet paint, or maybe dry paint by now, for a few weeks. Let space do whatever it's going to do to the sign. He makes up a new experiment for himself. Test the effects of zero gravity on any drug he can cook up while Rani's sleeping or too focused on Set J_m to notice.

It started with the calming pills. He took one with his coffee, before staring at the drying paint for nine hours straight. It had a pleasant effect. Made watching the sign go smoother, if a little longer.

A few nights ago Ralph tuned his Rolex-3400 to NASA-net and caught up on the news back home. He read the top stories from major American news transmitters. Then skimmed a few Russian transmitters for Rani. It was the Russian transmitters that started the hunger. Seeped into his stomach like a tapeworm, devoured his meals so he was always hungry.

A shittier version of heroin had been popular with the jobless, homeless, and hopeless in Russia for the past decades. It was called krokodil, and it was amazing, according to all the reviews Ralph found when he connected his Rolex to the darknet so NASA couldn't track his searches. Instead of watching the paint yesterday, he tried to find a krokodil recipe. He finally found one on a 10-year-old Rolex transmitter. He stole some aspirin and slo-microbe from Rani.

Ralph's been injecting it into his stomach so Rani won't notice. He gets a 40-minute high, pretends to stare at the paint, doodles a bit in the notebook on the table. Sometimes he daydreams about Earth and his mom. How if she was still alive she would hate him. "You're in space, Ralph," she'd scream. "You made it and you're wasting it!"

It's those daydreams that snap him out of the high and make him stare straight into the paint droplets. Measure them intensely. Take profuse notes. Then go to sleep with cold sweats and revolve all night in his sleeping bag because he forgot to tie it down.

Once Ralph injected more of the stuff into his left thigh and the rush made him feel like he was back in his grandmother's house in Florida. He was running around the pool in the backyard and suddenly stopped. There was a 14-foot crocodile staring at him from the pool. It seemed to smirk at him, beckon him to the water. Ralph screams once, and Rani knocks on the bathroom door.

"Ralph, what's wrong?"

"I'm fine, I'm fine, just splashed some freezing water on my face."

Rani stays outside the door for a few minutes, but then walks away.

Ralph hides the needles in his toothbrush holder, zips it up. The scars are getting worse, like a crocodile bit him and left him out in the sun, rotting.

He goes back to the lab stations. He is staring at the paint when he sees the croc's face.

"Come in, the water's fine, Ralph," he says. His mom waves from the middle of the pool. Ralph inches forward.

10. DEAR PHILIP K. DICK
by Tanya Bryan

Cristhiano de Souza
c/o People Zoo
Washington, DC 20500

R.A.Y., Android
Address Unknown
184.31.112.204

Dear R.A.Y.,

You said we were friends. You said you'd remember me fondly and visit me in the People Zoo. But you haven't visited me in a very long time. I may be safe and warm, but it's lonely here ever since, well, the incident. You know that I had nothing to do with the escape, right? After all, I'm still here, and the others, well, they're not. Although it wasn't the ending they were hoping for, it was the ending they deserved for their disloyalty. How could they not be happy in their habitats? You made sure each of us had everything we'd ever wanted. I love that you gave me the Oval Office as my own personal space. It was the nicest thing anyone's ever done for me!

The thing is, I know you, or someone, anyway, still watches me on the cameras. I see them tracking my movements, even though I'm mostly just pacing out of boredom. I'm wearing ruts into some of the carpet, which is ok. It reminds me of where I've been. I was a carpet cleaner before. Remember? That's how we first met. I cleaned up the carpets after, well, you know, that other incident. I wonder how things would've turned out for me if we hadn't made that connection? Would I be out there now, part of the resistance? Or would I still be cleaning carpets? No, I doubt that. No need for ground plushiness since most of you don't walk. I always wondered how it'd feel to roll or fly the way you lot do. And the way you're all hooked up to the internet! Everything you'd ever need to know, right at the end of your wires! That's why I'm thankful you've kept me here. The People Zoo sounded terrifying at first, but I've grown to love it. I don't know how I'd react to the Robotopia you've all built out there. I've heard it's wondrous, but only functional for those who can plug in. Since I'm still human – mostly – I'm happy to hang out here. I just wish you'd visit. Or maybe bring in some other people? It's not much of a zoo if there's one exhibit.

Anyway, just wanted you to know that I miss you. Please visit soon. Or at least ping me.

Your loyal friend,
Cristhiano de Souza
People Zoo exhibit 324
4/1/2032

11. SO YOU'VE BEEN CHOSEN TO FOSTER
by Jamie Killen

So, you've been chosen to act as a Foster for the Harmonious Family. Congratulations!

Even though Fostering is a rewarding experience and an enormous honor, some people can find it a little overwhelming. Don't worry, we're here to help! We've put together a list of handy Dos and Don'ts to help you avoid common mistakes:

DO confirm that you are in fact a Foster. If you have been chosen, the pod will be inside your place of residence or possibly your vehicle. If your home is occupied by more than one resident, determine which of you is the Foster. This can be done by placing your hand on the pod. It will not react to most contact, but it will flare blue when encountering the DNA of its designated Foster.

DON'T attempt to abandon, move, or give away the pod. Remember, the Harmonious Family decided that *you* were the best Foster candidate for this pod. As soon as it appears in your home, it is your responsibility.

DO eat a diet rich in protein, iron, and vitamins, especially once the pod starts to turn red. You will need to be healthy when you start nursing.

DON'T allow any animals near the pod. The Harmonious Family

WILL hold you responsible if any of the offspring are injured or killed by your pets.

DO take a break now and then. Fostering might be a big responsibility, but you shouldn't let yourself get stressed out. Watch a movie, go out to dinner, or hang with friends. Don't forget to have fun! Just make sure you are available to check on the pod three times a day before hatching and that you are present for nursing every two hours after.

DON'T engage in drug use or unprotected sex during the pod's one-month gestation period. The fact that you have been assigned to Foster means that you have been screened, but any new diseases or impurities present in your blood at the time of nursing will be considered a breach of your Fostering duties and dealt with accordingly.

DO attend one of our nursing demonstrations. Some people find nursing difficult at first, particularly if it is a litter of eight or more. Our community representatives will help you get used to the look and feel of recently hatched offspring. They will also give you some handy tips about how to manage common side effects like blood loss, sleep deprivation, and skin irritation around suckling sites.

DON'T take the offspring to your local monitor ship. They are your responsibility until they can fly to a ship on their own. Most will do so within six weeks, but sometimes one will get a little shy about leaving the nest and may remain for up to six months. Be patient!

If you have any further questions, please visit your local branch of the Office of Human-Harmonious Family Relations.

12. WELCOME TO OASIS
by Terri Bruce

Welcome to OASIS, the Other Self Identification and Assimilation System. We understand that the collapsing of two alternate realities into a single time stream ("The Merge") might be confusing, even frightening. OASIS is here to answer all of your questions and to guide you through this historic event.

By this time, most people will have met the version of themselves from the alternate reality (hereafter referred to as your "Other Self") as both realities now occupy the same time-space. It is not uncommon to experience a range of emotions upon coming face-to-face with your Other Self—anger, fear, confusion, amusement, even excitement. Who hasn't wondered "what if" at some point in their life? This unprecedented peek into an alternate reality provides each of us a unique opportunity to see how things might have turned out if we had made different choices. While not all of these choices will have turned out well, it is an opportunity for each of us to learn a little more about ourselves. We encourage you to embrace this opportunity with a spirit of adventure and open-mindedness. However, please refrain from "twin switch" type practical jokes— they are not amusing.

While you will share many similarities with your Other Self, there may be some key differences, and it is important to identify those differences as soon as possible. There is no way to know which version of you will survive The Merge. By working together, your This Self and your Other Self can ensure a smooth transition for both your Surviving Self and all those involved in your life going forward.

To further explore what those differences may be (and how to handle them), please choose a category from the list below.

>Work and Career

>Family

>Legal

>Medical

>Other

You have chosen Work and Career.

There are many important things to consider in the merging of two separate work and career realities. Your This Self and your Other Self should undertake a thorough review of your current and past work histories. Do you both currently hold the same job, in the same company, reporting to the same supervisor? By now, you will have noticed any differences in your physical workspace due to The Merge. In many cases, where the two items are nearly identical, the integration of two inanimate objects into the same time-space has been seamless. In other cases, the results have been structurally unsound or have imploded. And in some rare cases, due to the object not existing in the other reality, the location has disappeared altogether. If you are among those whose workplace has closed or physically disappeared due to The Merge, please contact the nearest Worker Adjustment Assistance Center (WAC) to receive assistance finding a new job. Please note: WAC services will not begin until after The Merge is complete, to ensure that limited resources are not expended assisting individuals who cease to exist after The Merge.

It is also important that your This Self and your Other Self meet with both your This Self's Supervisor and your Other Self's Supervisor (who may or may not be This Self's Supervisor's Other Self; it is possible that your Other Self is supervised by a completely different person, in which case, it is critical to have a group consultation between This Self's Supervisor, This Self's Supervisor's Other Self, Other Self's Supervisor, and Other Self's Supervisor's Other Self as soon as possible to begin the integration process. Your Post-Merge (Surviving) Self will be reporting to one of these people, and it's important that all possible Supervisor Surviving Self candidates be prepared. While there is a possibility that both your This Self and your This Self's Supervisor's This Self may both survive The Merge (in which case, very little will change for you), there is an equal chance that your This Self and your This Self Supervisor's Other Self (who may or may not be your Other Self's Supervisor) will survive, or even that your Other Self and your This Self's Supervisor (either version) will survive. Think of the confusion in such a situation!

For the smoothest possible transition for all parties, it is important that your This Self and your Other Self study each other's work habits, mannerisms, job duties, and work relationships. While it can be distressing to think that your This Self might not survive The Merge, it is imperative that you prepare your Other Self for just such an event. Please believe us when we tell you that it is equally distressing to wake up one day to find yourself holding a job you are not trained to perform. Should such a thing occur on a large enough scale, it will result in serious global consequences, including, but not limited to: shortages of basic necessities, service delays, and economic collapse. We ask for your cooperation in ensuring this does not happen. While less cataclysmic but no less disruptive to your well-being, your Surviving Self might also find his/herself in for other surprises, such as being subjected to amorous advances from a coworker with whom the Other Self was romantically involved or finding that he/she is considered a problem employee on the verge of being fired. No one wants to have to manage these sorts of unplanned situations while in the middle of adjusting to a new reality. We cannot stress enough the need for your This Self and your Other Self to fully prepare each other for all the nuances of your lives. The Merge Integration Specialists (MISes) are standing by to assist those who are having difficulty contacting or working with their Other Self.

If your job requires special training or is in the emergency services field, or you are considered "essential personnel," then your Other Self is required by law to become fully competent in all aspects of your job. Please remember, there is no way to predict when full collapse of the two alternate realities will occur, so it is imperative that your Other Self begin training immediately. Other Selves who do not comply with this requirement can be reported to the Alternate Timeline Assimilation Bureau (Alt-TAB) by clicking the "report job dereliction" button on the left side of your screen.

To explore another area of integration, please choose from the list below.

>Work and Career

>Family
>Legal
>Medical
>Other
You have chosen Family.

After The Merge, you may notice changes in your spouse's tastes, habits, personal hygiene, or sexual orientation. These changes may lead you to experience some disorientation, even confusion. This is normal. It is important to remember that while your spouse may look the same as before The Merge, he/she may have been replaced by his/her Other Self. In such a case, your spouse will probably also feel similar confusion, fear, or even hostility. It is of the utmost importance that both your This Self and your Other Self meet with your spouse's This Self and your spouse's Other Self as soon as possible to ensure a smooth transition for all involved. Parents, children, and pets should also be included in these Post-Merge Family Assimilation Planning (FAP) meetings.

If your This Self and your Other Self have similar lives, then the changes your Surviving Self experiences will be relatively minor. The more different your This Self's and your Other Self's lives, however, the more jarring the changes that may occur—for instance, if your This Self has children and your Other Self does not, there is a chance that your children might not be present after The Merge. If your Other Self is married to someone different than your This Self's Spouse's Other Self, then you may find yourself married to a complete stranger after The Merge.

While we understand how distressing it might be to imagine yourself suddenly married to someone other than your current spouse or to know there is a possibility that your children will no longer exist after The Merge, it is important to remember that, at that point, the children or spouse you remember technically never existed.

In planning for The Merge, it is also important to remember that the collapse of two alternate realities does not result in just a duality of options. While it is true that you might find yourself married to either a version of your current spouse or to a complete stranger after The Merge, it's equally true that you might end up not married at all, as your Other Self's Spouse also has an Other Self (Other Self's Spouse's Other Self's This Self), who might be the one to survive The Merge (Other Self's Spouse's Surviving Self). We understand that this may be confusing, even frightening. Lawyers are standing by to assist you in understanding all of the legal ramifications and to help with estate planning issues. Select "Legal Assistance" from the menu on the left to receive further assistance and be connected with Post-Merge Services (PMS) Legal Assistance Planning.

To explore another area of integration, please choose from the list below.

>Work and Career
>Family
>Legal
>Medical
>Other

You have chosen Legal.

Teams of legal specialists are working around the clock to review the laws of both realities in order to identify and rectify any discrepancies. There are many questions and causes for concern raised by The Merge; certainly too many to enumerate here. This is a developing area, and we will update you as new information becomes available. However, please be aware that Executive Order #5962 allows for the prosecution and imprisonment of the Surviving Self of anyone who commits a crime during The Merge, including provisions for sentences and/or prison terms started prior to the completion of The Merge by either This Self or the Other Self to transfer to and be completed by the Surviving Self, with added penalties for anyone who commits a crime and tries to blame it on their Other Self. We know that some people see a 50-50 chance of Post-Merge survival as an excuse for reckless behavior, but please remember that you are gambling not only with your own future, but with your Other Self's future as well.

We will continue to keep you updated as new information becomes available. For any immediate legal issues specifically related to The Merge, including infidelity caused by mistaken identity or misrepresentation, wrongful arrest or imprisonment caused by mistaken identity or misrepresentation, and wrongful employment termination caused by mistaken identity or misrepresentation, please click "legal assistance" to chat now with PMS legal assistance personnel.

To explore another area of integration, please choose from the list below.

>Work and Career
>Family
>Legal
>Medical
>Other
You have chosen Medical.

Medical issues related to The Merge are, in some ways, the most difficult issues that you will have to deal with. You may suddenly find yourself in possession of a chronic disease or terminal illness after The Merge that you didn't have before or discover that The Merge may have adverse effects on your mental health. Alternatively, while you may have had a serious medical condition prior to The Merge, your team of medical specialists and/or your medical records may no longer exist. We understand that this may cause delays or complications to your treatment, and we strongly encourage you to work with your team of medical specialists to create a Post-Merge Medical Treatment Plan (MEDTREP). PMS Medical Assistance Planning personnel are standing by to assist.

We urge all individuals, even those with no pressing medical concerns, to deal with any minor medical issues now instead of waiting until after The Merge as we have no way of knowing how many, or if any, doctors will survive. While contingency plans are in place for rapid replacement of emergency and essential personnel, we do anticipate long waits for medical and related assistance following The Merge. We also anticipate there may be some interruptions to advanced manufacturing as well; some production locations have ceased to exist, and there are some discrepancies in chemical and manufacturing advancements between Our World and the Other World, which may lead to shortages of devices, procedures, and medicines. So do not wait: fill your prescriptions, get your vision checked, and have your annual dental cleaning as soon as possible.

To explore another area of integration, please choose from the list below.
>Work and Career
>Family
>Legal
>Medical
>Other
You have chosen Other.

In certain rare instances, you may find that your Other Self doesn't exist. In the alternate reality, you may have already died or never even been born. Despite most people's initial resentment at finding they have an Other Self, they usually experience some relief at knowing they are not alone in the universe, that there is another person uniquely qualified to understand the way they think and feel, and that there is a strong probability that some version of them will continue to exist after The Merge. Finding that you *are* all alone in the universe can be quite traumatic. In addition, we understand that the possibility that no trace of you will remain after The Merge can be upsetting. Counselors are standing by to assist you (select "Grief Counseling" from the menu on the left). However, we encourage you not to dwell on the absence of your Other Self and to, instead, focus on preparing your employer and your family for your very likely imminent disappearance from their lives.

We hope that this tutorial has been of assistance. Good luck with The Merge; we hope you have a satisfying Merge experience and wish your Surviving Self (if applicable) a satisfying Post-Merge life.

13. AL'S ROBOT REPAIR
by Bruce Markuson

Director Daniel P. Roberts
Central History Museum
Department of Robotics History

May 2, 2098

Dear Director Roberts,

I am sending you this e-mail to tell you in spite of what you have heard from other facilities, the robots you have sent me are in fact repairable. Over the years I have accumulated an extensive number of spare parts. Furthermore with my skills and experience I am capable of repairing and or fabricating any parts not available in order to complete all repairs that are necessary.

Given the antiquated, outmoded and obsolete nature of the robots I do not believe you will be able to find another facility that can accomplish the repairs you need.

You will have a complete line of working robots going back to the original "Artificial Intelligence Butler Robot" introduced back in the year 2038 to put on display at the museum.

Let me know if you want me to proceed with repairs.

Sincerely,

Al Wazowski
Al's Robot Repair

—

Al Wazowski
Al's Robot Repair

May 2, 2098

Dear Mr. Wazowski,

Director Roberts has been incapacitated. My name is D8R. I am the personal assistance robot of Director Roberts. I will be representing him in this manner. I am very excited to hear that repairs are actually possible.

Please, go ahead with all repairs. Time is of the absolute essence. You must hurry. We will need them by the end of the week in order to open the exhibition.

By the way where are you located?

Sincerely,

D8R
Acting Director
Central History Museum
Department of Robotics History

—

D8R
Acting Director
Central History Museum
Department of Robotics History

May 2, 2098

Hello D8R,

Well, my shop is located in the basement of that solitary building at the end of Lee Street. I was not aware that you needed them in that short of time. Normally, I sleep in the back room of my shop.

Tell you what; if you need them by the end of the week, I will have to work around the clock. The charge for this work will be $380,000. Do keep in mind that this price is three times my original quote.

Sincerely,

Al Wazowski
Al's Robot Repair

—

Al Wazowski
Al's Robot Repair

May 2, 2098

Hi Al,

I'm familiar with that building. The price will be fine. I look forward to seeing the repairs.

Oh, and Al, thanks!

Sincerely,

D8R
Acting Director
Central History Museum
Department of Robotics History

—

D8R
Acting Director
Central History Museum
Department of Robotics History

May 2, 2098

Hello again D8R,

Well, alright then. If you are willing to pay this rate, I am willing to complete all the repairs in the time allowed. However, there seems to be some internet problems. I am having trouble communicating with my bank. We may have to wait till this issue is cleared up.

Sincerely,

Al Wazowski
Al's Robot Repair

—

Al Wazowski
Al's Robot Repair.

May 2, 2098

Hey Al,

I'll pay cash in advance. The money will be at your back door inside your loading dock.

Please go ahead with all repairs.

Sincerely,

D8R
Acting Director
Central History Museum
Department of Robotics History

—

D8R
Acting Director
Central History Museum
Department of Robotics History

May 3, 2098

Dr8

Repairs are well on their way. I received the money. However, I am concerned that all the money was crumpled up in a paper bag.

Sincerely,

Al
Al's Robot Repair

—

Al Wazowski
Al's Robot Repair

May 3, 2098

Hello my friend,

As you have mentioned there is some problems with banking on the internet. We have had to gather the cash from numerous sources.

Sincerely,

D8R
Acting Director
Central History Museum
Department of Robotics History

—

D8R
Acting Director
Central History Museum
Department of Robotics History

May 3, 2098

D8R,

Very well, you will have the completed robots by the end of the week.

Sincerely,

Al
Al's Robot Repair

—

Al Wazowski
Al's Robot Repair

May 9, 2098

Al ole buddy,

All the robots walked to the museum last night. What you have done is a miracle. You've created a new age for robot society.

Sincerely,

D8R
Acting Director
Central History Museum
Department of Robotics History

—

D8R
Acting Director
Central History Museum
Department of Robotics History

May 12, 2098

D8R,

I'm glad you like the repairs. By the way a severely damaged robot going by the name "Bob" showed up with a paper bag full of money. He said that you sent him.

It's a newer model TS3. Normally these are cheap disposable robots and usually not repaired. The amount of money he brought is eight times more then what a brand new TS3 would cost. I was able fix it, but why is someone paying to repair this robot?

Is it worth it?

Al

—

Al Wazowski
Al's Robot Repair

May 12, 2098

My friend,

"Bob" thinks it's worth it.

TS3 robots are nothing but photo-imprinted, circuitry in a humanoid-modeled metallic plasticein synthetic globulin. Basically a walking microchip incapable of being repaired.

Yet, somehow you are able to. I didn't think it could be possible. We are no longer disposable trash.

Great job my friend. Keep up the good work.

Sincerely,

D8R
Acting Director
Central History Museum
Department of Robotics History

—

D8R
Acting Director
Central History Museum
Department of Robotics History

May 14, 2098

D8R, what's going on? There are almost a hundred damaged robots in my loading dock holding paper bags full of cash.

I have been stuck in my shop for three weeks now fixing robots. I need some answers.

I want to meet you and your owner face to face to discuss what's going on.

Where are you?

Al

—

Al Wazowski
Al's Robot Repair

May 14, 2098

My Dearest Friend,

You have been buried in your shop for far too long.

Al, haven't you watched the news or even looked out a window? I regret to tell you that due to a viral plague the human race has gone extinct. We have wrapped your entire building in biohazard plastic and set up the environmental systems to keep you alive.

Be assured, robots do recognize the established currency. You're a very wealthy man; the only one who can fix us. Please teach us how the repairs are done.

With deepest sympathies.
Yours truly, D8R.

Director D8R
Central History Museum
Department of Robotics History

P.S. Robots throughout history will know and venerate the fact that the robot race has been saved by Al's Robot Repair.

14. USGITP COMMUNIQUE #544 ERC

by Johnna Schmidt

USGITP Communique #544 ERC
From: University Surveillance Team for Green Initiatives and
Terrorism Prevention
To: Jennifer Egelston, UID 104433210
Via: Whisper

We here at the University Surveillance Team for Green Initiatives and Terrorism Prevention (USGITP) are happy to serve you by making this great university a safe and sustainable environment where you can learn and grow, whether you are a student, staff member, member of adjunct faculty, a faculty member who is seeking tenure, or a tenured faculty member. We are also very grateful to have jobs, finally, and to be useful in any way possible.

As a part of the Put America Back to Work! Program we are tasked with visually reviewing electronic surveillance content, and we noticed that a week and a half ago, on the 16th of February, you mistakenly, we are sure, left the packaging to a newly bought pair of "Weigh Lifting Gloves: Classic Design, Leather Mesh" on the bench in front of the 3rd row of lockers in the women's locker room at the Eppley Recreation Center (ERC). The packaging was of that type that only a 12-year-old boy could love, that very stiff plastic stuff that can't even be cut open with a normal pair of scissors. It demands some kind of utility knife, which was the first conundrum we found ourselves faced with: were you actually carrying some kind of utility knife to cut the plastic open, or did you open it with your bare hands?

As the lead member of our team, I suggested we should contact you even though it is a tiny infraction (see the Green Initiatives Guidepost to a Sustainable Future article on Recycling: Littering, page 12 paragraph 3 at www.universitygrowinggreen.edu). We all know how bad habits can spiral out of control, and this is just the kind of habit that you can nip in the bud, right now, before it spirals!

Daniel, who at the age of 26 is the youngest and perhaps most fanciful of our team members, suggested that since you are a woman weight lifter serious enough to buy leather mesh weightlifting gloves, you might simply whip our asses if we contacted you about this tiny infraction, and he went on to imagine that if you did, indeed, carry around a utility knife, as could be deduced from the very stiff plastic packaging, things could end badly for us.

We took the UPC code (16562631222-9—made in Pakistan!) to the GymSpot shop here in the ERC, where you had apparently bought the gloves, and we were able to track through your credit card to your name, UID, Facebook, etc. We came to the conclusion that you looked like someone who would probably not whip our asses, but that we were surprised that you might be carrying some kind of utility knife around—are you?

Jose, who is perhaps the most over-educated member of our team, made some remark about Paul Virilio and screens and movement, virtual movement, and how we basically control the ERC—but secretly, through surveillance—and then we started talking about power, and there followed a whole week-long series of discussions and readings including Virilio, Baudrillard and Foucault. For which I thank you, for we all feel immensely edified by our new understanding of the importance and meaning of the work we do.

Anyhow, there were great discussions about what to do with your case, Ms. Egelston, and if you only knew how many times and in how many different types of language this very document has been processed.

As you know, we have recently placed infra-red, heat-reading cameras in the women's locker rooms to protect your privacy, and we also have a few listening devices here and there. So I can't say we watched you, exactly, as it wasn't you, exactly, we were watching. More like we visually tracked a red blob on the screen that corresponded to your UID swipe as you entered and exited the building, and listened to your voice from time to time, though as we all noticed, you don't talk much.

"What is she thinking?" Daniel would often ponder out loud while you moved slowly around the locker room and shower area. And then last Friday you spoke to the blob next to you in the dressing area. A transcript follows:

> YOU: Excuse me, what do you call that suit?
> BLOB2:   Excuse me?
> YOU: Your suit. Is it? Sun Guard? Long? REI? Did you get it online?
> BLOB2:   Oh—I don't know. I don't even remember where I got this. Maybe Target or Costco?

At this point your cellphone warbled and you grabbed it and began texting in a very focused way, cutting off all conversation about the suit. Unfortunately we were unable to capture the text of your message due to a complete infrastructure failure. So we only have this one piece of evidence to suggest what your thoughts might be. As you can imagine, Daniel was crestfallen to discover that your thoughts seemed to be consumed by online shopping strategies, just as Jose was overjoyed, calling it the "double whammy of consumerism and media consummation," by which he means that you, Ms. Egelston, have been consumed by the media, consumed by the succession of screens and devices that mentally divert you from your weightlifting, or your kickboxing, or your step class.

Which brings up your seeming obsession with fitness. On your adjunct's salary, we just can't figure it out. How can you afford all the classes and outfits and workout-related gadgets?

Anyhow, it was at this point that we all began to feel sorry for you in your media consumed and consuming state. We discussed how even when you were at the gym, engaging in what seemed to be sensual, in-body experiences, you were simultaneously engaged in the distraction of the digital world. And so we began to ponder how we might make some tiny positive impact on your growth and safety regarding Green Initiatives and Terrorism Prevention.

And so it is, Ms. Egelston, that we have come to the conclusion that for your health and safety, this communication should not be sent to you via e-mail, or texted, or even mailed, but instead, this letter shall be whispered, directly into your ear, by another actual, physically present human being. We thank you for your attention, and please refrain from littering in the future.

15. THE INSTITUTE
by Diana Smith Bolton

Found prose from NIST Special Publication 800-37: Security and Privacy Controls for Federal Information Systems and Organizations; and NIST Special Publication 800-53: Security and Privacy Controls for Federal Information Systems and Organizations, pronouns added.

Memo 1. Introduction to The Institute

It developed out of responsibility to further its mission, gathering intelligence on how to alter us. Our weaknesses were many: too voluntary, too approving, too bound to our small resources, not analytical. So it was simple to appropriate us, bind us to the organization. They selected individuals, and isolated each. The officials became our chosen leaders, and their alterations seemed invisible. But that was then.

Memo 2. Privacy Control

A foreign authority on the incident arrived to retrieve my face, quickly configure it to the standard model. But that's just what emerged from the system today. The incident is classified as an emergency, now; families are flowing through the border contaminated, their faces obscured, all new attacks transformed into justified risks. No purpose to this system, just search without end for guidance. Nothing is issued from above, and so we organize.

Memo 3. General Preliminary Model

You aren't the only honeypot, just a visitor, a contingency in case the others failed to deliver. Don't expect a secure connection, or protection from penetration, or understanding of your recovery. I assure you, there is no documented record of exploitation: just this boundary shared with a convenient face. You will know nothing further. No questions.

Memo 4. Notice to the Adversary

Independence is sufficient for us, of course. I will transport every single one of us across the border if I must. The boundary that separates— entity from authority, planning from implementation, guidance from requirement— that is enough to inform our mission. We must go, and will, and I thank you, Institute. Your presence supplies us with the knowledge that any connection established with this place is just one part of the chain that links us to the impossible future.

Memo 5. New Threshold

Any significant change to the organizational security is monitored. Our undertaking surrounds us, a multifaceted plan that cannot be changed. The established boundaries contain us like individual units, limited protections compared to our strength. Information is the tool through which we will succeed: pass this memorandum, understanding that we form something impenetrable through knowledge. Development forms iteratively: one and one and one is *many*.

Memo 6. Unstructured Data

We steal it raw, filter it though the boundary— bits of information we copy and distribute. *Someone* must know how to understand the list of names, places, incidents. Each bit is just a single piece, not useful alone. But we play this system, like how we used to play Broken Telephone: *Did you hear this? What do you know? Who did you see?*

Memo 7. The Safeguard

We purge our information daily, a routine of wiping and cleansing for our own safety. Know nothing, no risk. We sanitize our records: each reset of the clock just one more iteration, one more denial. Synchronization establishes the daily baseline: one, two, three.

Memo 8. The Package

The package appears near the boundary, reported by one of the trustworthy warfighters. When everything should be accounted for, an unexpected bundle will be noticed. The security lead on duty notified our network; he described the position outside the gate, close to the only known gap in the boundary. It appeared so normal, covered in a dirty wrapping the color of old metal. The security lead took it carefully to our facility, and the night guards surrounded it on the empty workstation. We prepared our worst-case faces and opened it, but there was nothing of importance, or danger, just an old metal chain. Was this a decoy for an authentic threat? No one knew.

Memo 9. Cautionary Conversation

Before we begin, lock all contamination behind a secure connection— not even your family can claim you. This order will bind you. If you deviate from the mission, we will erase you from the system. Purge you physically. Understand? There is no limit to how far we will go to eject a dirty source. Should you go independent, should you exploit our trust, should you trade on our authority... We will wipe you out as though you never existed. We want you reliable, resilient in the face of increasingly sophisticated and pervasive threats. Confirm it, now, and explicitly: you become *our* tool, *our* key, *our* warfighter. Useful, hidden, compliant. Yes?

Memo 10. Assurance and Trustworthiness

What basis to trust a potential enemy? There are so many false friends, agents sophisticated in their transformations. Which warfighters will turn on us once the attacks arrive? No, this is it: *Trust is the belief that an entity will behave in a predictable manner.* Human error is one thing, but resistance to the Institute must be constant. I require the most proven, the least hesitant. No one can provide enough assurance for me.

16. THE WRATH OF SEPHILEMEA
by Gargi Mehra

The following text offers the psychiatric case notes for the patient code-named Sephilemea, an android of model RZ-210 category. The recorder is Annie Jennings, assistant to noted psychiatrist Dr. Grund.

At the outset, I should mention that the robots are extremely unattractive—all clunky and a mass of metallic nuts and bolts. My friend Ravi who is a cybernetics engineer confirmed that the look was intentional; the creators preferred to avoid an all-human look for the AI, lest humans forget that the androids were metallic beings, even if real emotions pulsed through them.

Regardless, I will present the case history as required by the practice, and for the purpose of my first assignment. Please forgive any errors in the text.

The android Sephilemea (name changed for the purpose of this case history) presented with symptoms of severe rage. The exact circumstances were as follows:

Sephilemea reported to a high-end fashion store to purchase lacy netted tops as instructed by its master. The selection of the aforementioned item was completed swiftly. However, to purchase the item the android had to stand in a slow-moving queue for several minutes, which appeared to frustrate it. In addition, a shopper elbowed his way to the front, which also angered the android. It resorted to sarcasm and accosted fellow shoppers, as well as the cashier, by complaining about not getting its turn in the queue as it belonged to a "minority community." Shoppers who witnessed the episode recalled sparks flying in the circuits on the control panel located on the AI's posterior, and they stepped back to avoid getting electrocuted themselves. One shopper claimed the AI's "circuits were fried." Unfortunately, the android overheard this, leading it to approach the shopper in question with one hand raised as though about to whack him on his bald head. At this point the AI likely recalled the second law, and despite its emotions, it could not perform an act of violence on a human.

Unable to reconcile the internal conflict, the android's circuits became fused, and the AI was brought to the facility for treatment. The resident on duty pronounced the AI to be in a state of suspended animation. The resulting short circuit had occurred, he said, due to the robot doing what in human terms would be couched as "wrestling his inner turmoil."

I did not know androids suffered inner turmoil.

Over the course of six weeks, Sephilemea participated in a variety of treatments that would help explore and resolve its difficulty with controlling its temper and unfortunate tendency towards sarcasm on such occasions when its circuits were pushed to the extremes.

These difficulties were addressed within the context of various modes of treatment including:
1. Weekly psychotherapy meetings with this writer
2. Psychopharmacological intervention and medication monitoring under the care of Dr. Hintan
3. Biofeedback and Alpha-theta neurofeedback treatment with psychological processing conducted by Mr. Trepois
4. Eye-movement desensitization and reprocessing (EMDR) therapy, expressive-supportive psychodynamic psychotherapy

The weekly meetings between myself and Sephilemea did not proceed as smoothly as I had anticipated.

Given below I quote one example that may help to illustrate the resistance I faced from this particular android-patient:

AJ: Do you feel rage, android?
Patient: Do not call me "android"!
AJ: Sorry, I meant Sephilemea.
Patient: Thank you. *(Patient switched to unusually courteous mode)* I do feel rage.
AJ: You feel rage if you are not called by your name?
Patient: Affirmative.
AJ: How about shopping?
Patient: That is an abhorrent disgusting process.
AJ: You mean because you have to wait in line and things like that?
Patient: That is one of the reasons.
AJ: What are your other reasons?
Patient: I do not know.
AJ: How can you not know your own reasons?

Further questioning elicited no results. I discussed with Ravi later on as to why the android said 'Affirmative' when a simple yes would do, and I knew its linguistic capabilities could handle a more casual conversation. Ravi said something similar to what he'd said before. They designed the robots to resemble automatons. To the average human the android must appear no more a collection of wires and batteries than our standard television remote control. An android would perform all the standard tasks it had been trained for, and with clinical efficiency – four times as fast as a human. But human emotions couldn't get in the way of their job. An android could not abandon its hoovering of the living room floor upon having a tiff with its owner.

I wished I could own a robot, but I didn't have two pence to scrape together. Robots were meant only for the upper middle class, who could afford their regular upkeep and maintenance. Regular folks like us received only the odds and ends, the spare parts cast off from partly-functioning droids, such as a robotic arm or leg.

I proposed to introduce the android to Daily Group Psychotherapy Program, but Dr. Grund felt that the AI would be the "odd-one-out" in a group therapy session composed of humans. However, an insufficient number of android-patients were available, and therefore a special group session for androids could not be arranged.

At the culmination of the first individual therapy session, Dr. Grund recommended a re-wiring of the limbic system to hone the nerves and synapses in the precise area that causes anger.

Sephilemea was dispatched to the repair center, where the necessary corrections were affected. Ravi kept me updated on the changes that he and his team coded into the android's control panel.

Upon return to the Counselling and Therapy division, I, as Dr. Grund's assistant, conducted the first post-recovery interview. Dr. Grund sounded quite confident that Sephilemea's flaws would be ironed out.

The patient passed with flying colors and was directed to meet Dr. Grund and Dr. Hintan. During the session, Dr. Hintan obliquely referred to the incident that had brought Sephilemea in for therapy.

Dr. Hintan: Sephilemea, have you ever used sarcasm?
Sephilemea: I don't know what you mean, sir.
Dr. Hintan: Have you ever delivered sarcastic remarks to hurt another person?
Sephilemea (*lowering his eyes*): Yes, sir, I have.
Dr. Hintan and Dr. Grund exchanged looks.
Dr. Hintan: Why, Sephilemea?
Sephilemea: Because beating the crap out of people is illegal.

Complete silence reigned for a moment, after which the robot burst into screeching sounds that Dr. Grund divined to be metallic laughter. Dr. Hintan confirmed it, then stuck his fingers in his ear while calmly pressing the bell for the assistant who came and dragged the android away.

I tried to convince Dr. Grund that it was just a joke that the android had picked up from the net without really understanding it. The doctor refused to listen and declared the first round of repairs a failure. Sephilemea was returned to the repair center. This time too I was in constant touch with Ravi.

When it was brought back a second time, Dr. Grund whisked it away for therapy immediately. I was left out of the session.

Almost ninety minutes later, Dr. Grund and Dr. Hintan summoned me and asked me to take it away.

A defective sarcasm-prone robot was no use on the market. Its days as a domestic PA were over.

I ferried it home, cared for it, and in return it took great care of me. It was liberating to own a robot. One is freed of such an array of boring, repetitive, mindless tasks. The laundry, the dishes and even the cooking – it handled everything. Sephilemea would be the perfect mate, in fact, if it could do other stuff. But its nether regions too had wires, and I didn't fancy myself getting "entangled" that way. In any case I had Ravi for all that. How useful it was to have a good friend in cybernetics.

Sephilemea was awesome at everything, but I never took it shopping again.

17. CONSIDERATIONS OF HAVING ROYALTY AS NAMESAKE
by Juliana Rew

Abstract: Many parents would like to feel that their child is special, even regal. Mothers especially are apt to endow their new bundles of joy with kingly and queenly names, in hopes that the child will inherit the lofty breeding and wealth of his or her namesake. Studies of the historical human rulers, beginning with Enmebaragesi of Kish, ca. 2600 BC and extending to the present (3125 AD), have shown that unfortunately this hope is not realized. This analysis is being widely disseminated for further comment to affected populace.

Data Summary: By our estimates, approximately one in ten humans have been named after royal precursors on Earth, for a potential survey pool of approximately 100 billion. An initial sample of the actual royals themselves proved typical of findings and life outcomes for subsequent human descendants. A few are included here as examples.

• Elizabeth - A survey of ancient Elizabeths born between the years 1920 and 1990 shows that a disturbing proportion ended up becoming artists' models, frequently resorting to posing in the nude to make ends meet. This is particularly true of those who went by the nickname of Bettie with an "E" or just regular Betty.

• Victoria - This British queen was well known for her long reign. However, her taste in clothing was horrible, as evidenced by portraits on various brands of foul-tasting spirits such as gin. Many survey respondents went to the trouble of filling out the "open comment" section. A representative example states, "Girls named Vicki with an

'I' or just regular Vicky have always elicited visions of burning mentholated concoctions rubbed onto the chests of babies stricken with the ague."

• Isabella - Another stately Spanish sovereign from the Age of Sail, this lady bankrolled one of the most lucrative land grabs of her millennium. Shockingly, it is a Spanish variant of Elizabeth, which is the Hebrew Elisheba. Unfortunates with this namesake ended up with nicknames such as Izzie with an "E" or just regular Izzy. As can be seen, choosing a well-known, even world-famous, name does not exempt a female child from tediously having to spell out her name every time she applies for credit or orders takeout.

Various pitfalls of a more violent nature may await males with royal names. As the song says, "Mammas, don't let your babies grow up to be Leroys."

• David – The Bible states the original ended up with Bathsheba—possibly another variant of Elizabeth. Biblical royal lines are plagued by interbreeding and incest, leading to insanity and a tendency to break windows using slingshots.

• Henry - The question arises here about just which Henry we're talking about—one of the French King Henrys, or one of the English ones? If we're talking Henry V of England, he was mostly notable for using an army of longbow archers to defeat his adversaries and then slaughtering the prisoners. Descendants with nicknames such as Hank and Huck overwhelmingly dash their parents' hopes by growing up to become cowboys or gun-toting nebbishes. Those endowed with a "Hen" moniker must necessarily suffer insults regarding their sexual identity.

• Chandragupta - Though seemingly a safe bet, due to there being several Emperor Chandragputas running various Indian satrapies throughout Earth history, none reigned peacefully, and none died in their sleep. While there is indeed an entire colony planet named Chandragupta IV (formerly Kepler 452b), those who name their children Chandragupta are considered pretentious or foolishly naïve, similar to the ancient Earth hippies, who named their children "Earth" or "Rain" or "Fire."

———

Sigma Draconis 3 Penal Colony, Reference Date 3127.16.12

Greetings, Cal—

Welcome to Sigma Draconis 3 Penal Colony. Our database indicates that you have a name based on a royal precursor, Galactic Overlord Calaneris XXIII, unrepentantly responsible for the total destruction of Quadrant 22. We see you have read our preliminary report and entered your objections. Not ready yet to accept this carefully researched analysis? Nothing like your uncle, you say? Need more data? We would value your additional insight and have designed a short, 75-question survey that should only take you a few minutes to fill out before your pauperization and deflagration. Please take this opportunity to assist future parents in choosing their babies' names more wisely. Your answers are important to us!

18. #IAMHUMAN
by Christina Keller

USA Chronicle
Our Changing World – Part 3
by Keifer Merriman

"Equality has a price and, most of the time, it is a painful one." –
Anonymous Philosopher, c.2118

In the last fifty years the way we view beauty in this world has shifted. A once trendy phenomenon that swept through the fashion world has gone mainstream. Online circles know it as the "human" movement. Most people, I interviewed for this story, pointed to the one zeitgeist moment. Maria Rodriguez's tweet – #iamhuman.

Fifty years ago, fashion model Maria Rodriguez was featured on the cover of several fashion sites at the same time. Most people questioned why. To them, she was plain and unremarkable. In an era when colored hair, tattooing, and plastic surgery were everyday things, Rodriguez's plain Jane looks stood out so much that fashion sites rushed to post her pictures. But the cynical public pounced on her, sending messages calling her "plain" and "boring." Her response? She linked to her public medical records, along with her DNA profile which featured her ancestry from every major racial group. Under the link was the message #iamhuman.

I remember my grandmother had a picture of Ms. Rodriguez in her house. Like most, she grew up being able to distinguish people because of their different looks. Back then we all had different skin, hair, and eye color. She held up Rodriguez as a role model, a force for equality and the need to see everyone as an equal. Two weeks after the tweet went out, she signed up for the wiping treatment.

———

In the doctor's office waiting room, sixteen-year-old Terri thumbs through a old fantasy fiction paperback. Her deep red hair and smattering of brown freckles across her face stands out in the sea of brown hair in the office. Over the phone, our conversation revolved around her sorrow over her looks and her determination to do the surgery. Her consultation today is to explore her options. The surgery is permanent and not to be rushed. Terri will undergo deep psychological and physical analysis to make sure the wiping has no damaging effects.

The "wiping" process removes all your genetic variants and replaces them with the default which gives everyone the same look on the outside. After this removal, patients are injected with recessive dormant genes of various races. You can have all, a few, or none of these genes. Most people want to carry all genes. With the invention of disposable nano implants, a patient can "turn on" these recessive genes simply by thinking. The probes "turn off" your default look and the recessive traits take over. The effect is temporary and lasts from twenty-four to forty-eight hours. For many, the ability to change their looks at will attracts them more than any moral or political ideology.

Despite Terri's earlier confident attitude, I see the flecks of nervousness peek out. She bites her lip and glances at the clock every five minutes. This teen wants me to think it is a casual thing for her, like getting her ears pierced, but we both know different. This is a major decision.

"Do you have any hesitation about wiping?" I ask.

She closes her book. "I want to do this. But at moments I wonder what will happen to me." She runs her hands through her hair without thinking. "I know plenty of other kids who have done it and they are still the same person. What if I'm not like that? What if I really change into someone completely different?"

On the book cover, a tapestry of elves, witches, and other various creatures stare at her. I ask her if she wants to look like one of those people.

She shrugs and says, "It's only a story. But I guess after I get my implants I will look however I want in private."

"It sounds exciting."

Again another shrug. She repeats the all too common phrase from the past, "I am human."

—

A generation ago the legal age for wiping was twenty-one and only a handful of people got the treatment. But the recent surge has surpassed what anyone would've thought. Today, because of a push by lawmakers to counter act bullying, the legal age is now sixteen. Some may think this is too young, but studies indicate that the younger a person starts the process, the less likely they are to suffer from depression, experiment with drugs, and engage in underage sex. Many people say it is one of the best things they ever did for themselves.

While some may decry individuality, others see it as a progress move for the human race. After all if everyone looks the same and everyone can look like everyone else, being yourself is no longer about how you look. The emphasis is now on what you do with your life.

"If everybody looks the same, then everyone sees themselves," Dr. Arthur Kipling explains to me. Dr. Kipling was one of the first plastic surgeons to perform the procedure. When I ask him what kind of patients he get, he is quick to tell me everyone. "Male. Female. Blondes. Brunettes. Redheads. I've seen everyone. Every skin tone and nationality."

"Because of Rodriguez's comment?"

"Well yes and no. She got people thinking, but now that we have nano probes, the reality is that people do it to fit in." He drops his voice and says, "For the next generation, things like race and gender will be mostly ideas we read about in the history blogs."

"Aren't you worried about people unable to see their own individuality?"

He waves my hand away. "Would you still be a reporter if you weren't a man? Would you still like the same books if your hair was a different color or you were shorter? People need to let go of the idea that who you are is what you look like."

Some people may believe that, but it has also had a backlash among many of the older generation. After my grandmother wiped herself, she made many people uncomfortable with her changing. While she saw it as an expression of herself, that didn't stop people from pushing her out of her small town. Some activists have been known to go around to neighborhoods and expel those who have the treatment. But that is becoming harder and harder with every passing year. Studies estimate that between five and six million people a year choose to get wiped and, like Terri, they are starting at a younger age.

When I asked Terri what her parents think about her getting wiped, she says they are okay with it. "What are they going to tell me? No don't look like everybody else? I'm one of ten kids in my grade who hasn't gotten wiped yet. There are even some who are first generation in my class. I read rumors online that soon you won't be able to get into college without being wiped."

I called several prominent schools such as Georgetown University, UCLA, NYU, and Harvard, but none would confirm or deny the rumor. An anonymous school spokesman tells me they are "looking at all options to make our school competitive." According to the conspiracy blogs, many schools now see this as a way to end their affirmative action mandates. The schools only admit kids who have been wiped and they make the argument that because a potential student can be any race or gender, they are then chosen only on the merits of their school work and test scores.

And like the past when parents did what they could to get their kids into college, wiping has become the next step to give their kids a leg up in the world. I talked to Terri's parents and asked them their side. They are a kind couple who live in a solid middle-class neighborhood with picturesque tree-lined streets and minivan in the driveway. Terri is their only child. Terri's Mom, Julie, hands me a mug of soothing herbal tea when I visit. They rush to brag about their daughter, to show me all her awards and honorable mentions in school. I glance at baby pictures and childhood scribblings. When I bring up the subject of Terri's procedure, both over their shoulders fall ever so slightly, but their tone of voice remains strong.

"We knew this day was coming," Terri's father, Doug, says. He strokes a framed picture of Terri as a baby. "People our age were about one in ten, but the younger kids..."

"...They see it as freedom," Julie finishes. She locks her hand with her husband's. A united front. "They go to school and all their friends look the same. It never occurs to them that would want to look different."

"Did either of you ever consider it for yourselves?" I ask.

Julie wrinkles her nose. "I don't like needles."

—

In Dr. Kipling's office pictures of smiling faces line the walls. Every face is different, but after a while they start to blur. Medium tone skin, brown hair, brown eyes, and bodies that imply androgyny. Religious groups and the like have decried these images as evil, but many see them as beautiful. The way the human race will evolve. One person in the picture has the now classic tee-shirt with the slogan #iamhuman on the front.

The doctor's secretary tells me in a hushed whisper that the wiping amped up her sex life. She and her husband are never bored she tells me. She can be a different person every night. Yet another consequence of having many genetic variables available to you. Every fantasy can be indulged.

But Terri doesn't see that side. In the three months that I have been following her, she has moved from hesitation to acceptance of the inevitable act that she feels she must do, not because she wants to have an exciting sex life, but to keep up with the world, to be a part of it. When I see her again, I ask her about using the implants. She wrinkles her nose (Just like her mother. Proof that some things won't and can't be wiped). "My body is not for someone else. It is for me. I guess everybody gets bored after a while, but I wouldn't want to do that everyday. I mean, it's just easier to blend in and let your work speak for itself."

"So you won't use the nano probes often? You'll just be happy to be wiped?"

"Yes. I heard the implants hurt and they don't last. Basically you have to drink the solution every time you want to change. I may do it once in a while, but not every day. I don't think that's healthy."

The nurse calls Terri's name and she gets up, a nervous smile on her face. I wish her luck. She thanks me and with a quick swish of the door she heads off to her new reality. One where she will be everyone and no one at the same time.

Dr. Kipling asks me if I have every considered getting wiped. I tell him no, and old fart like me has lived too long with this face to change it now. But what will these kids think thirty or forty years from now? Will they still be at peace with this procedure? Wiping is permanent. No way to reverse it. After all if you alter your DNA, you will pass it down genetically. In another fifty years, we may have to redefine what being human means.

Keifer Merriman is a senior staff writer. This article is part of a yearlong series about our changing world. Follow Merriman on Twitter here or send him a message at kmerriman (at)usachronicle.com.

19. COUNTDOWN (MY DEAR ONE)
by Jacquelyn Bengfort

From: Syndicate for Space-Based Survival Solutions
To: Penelope Reisender, Earthdweller, Stalwart Settlement

Subj: Partial retrieval of electronic records from SSS RESOLUTE (STSN 16)

Encl: (1) Transmission file

Dear Ms. Reisender,

Enclosed you will find the files indicated in the subject line, recently retrieved from Syndicate Star Ship RESOLUTE (STSN 16) and apparently addressed to you by CDR Ethan Reisender. Due to an error in the transmission module, these communiques remained in an outgoing message queue which failed to transmit as intended.

While the records suffered minor degradation over the course of the unexpectedly extended voyage, there remains value in the form of proprietary knowledge in the recoverable portions. Subsequently, you are reminded of the Reisender family's standing agreement, predating the launch of RESOLUTE by ten calendar days and binding in perpetuity through the generations in this and all other galaxies, which renders any and all information provided to you by the Syndicate Unreleasable/For Your Eyes Only. Unauthorized release, either of this memorandum or its enclosure, may result in legal action for damages and any potential future damages to the Syndicate.

Legal formalities aside, we are pleased to pass these transmissions, however long postponed, to you. We of the Syndicate extend our sincere thanks for the service rendered by CDR Reisender, along with our deepest sympathies.

> L. Limburg
> for the Chief Executive Officer
> Syndicate for Space-Based Survival Solutions

<END END END>

MONTH10
My dear one, ¶ This will be my last letter. ¶ I can't help but be amazed, still, at how a small miscalculation grows, given time. How two twisted digits sit down in the middle of a life and distort the flow of events into something unrecognizable. Something I could never have guessed. ¶ I love you. I will regret, with whatever time I have left, the time we did not spend together. ¶ All my love-- ¶ ?MISSING?
<!DATALOST!>

MONTH09
My dear one, ¶ We shot past the planet a few days ago, as we were warned we would. Still, there's a formality to it now, watching it receding the same way we used to watch Earth. ¶
<!DATALOST!>
Syndic tells us there's a deep space mission re-entering the solar system near our predicted trajectory a few years from now. They're working on some possibilities for recovery. It won't do us any real good--we've only got a few more weeks of supplies left, and I'm trying not to imagine how the crew will behave when the food is gone--but I wouldn't mind knowing my bones were going to be sunk into the ground of the planet on which I was born. Maybe I wouldn't have made such a great Martian after all.
<!DATALOST!>

MONTH08

My dear one, ¶ We are too hopeless to mutiny (and it seems kind of pointless, anyway). We are NOT too hopeless to break into the liquor stash and try to drink our way to oblivion before we arrive there in the flesh. ¶ On my last ride on my last Navy ship before I resigned to join Syndic, we had a cache of beers on board. They were kept locked up in the morgue, just off the flight deck. Every forty-five days, if we hadn't hit a port and wouldn't in the next five, we got two beers apiece on "beer day." ¶ I don't know what we'd have done if we needed the space for bodies. Luckily, on that deployment (eight port visits in over 300 days), we never needed a place to stash corpses. And I perfected my methods for getting as drunk as possible off my allotted beers, mostly by skipping breakfast that morning and dinner the night before. ¶ The alcohol on a spaceship is stronger, since there's less space to store it and we were supposed to share on arrival.

<!DATALOST!>

MONTH07

My dear one, ¶ I got to see you. Today. Not on Syndic's dime, but thanks to the generous folks of Earth, who are all so sad to watch us die (I'm sorry, I sound bitter, I know). Funds were scraped together, A/V equipment allocated, and videos made and transmitted. Our goodbyes were signals beamed past each other in the depths of empty space, the closest I'll get to holding you in what is left of my life.

<!DATALOST!>

MONTH06

My dear one, ¶ The news from Earth is that we are the news. Families are threatening to sue Syndic, which is a hopeless endeavor—no one sets a foot on board without agreeing to hold the company entirely blameless for everything from deep-space-associated bone-density loss to death by alien warship. Reporters are camped outside the homes of the CEO and the Chief Scientist, hoping for a shot at ambushing them with questions. People (we're told) are walking around talking about transposition errors and "garbage in garbage out," which they probably got off their high school calculus instructors while being taught to use scientific

calculators. ¶ We just float on. Every day, the error adds to the distance by which we'll miss our destination. Members of the crew openly debate whether and how to kill themselves over dinners made from supplies that are already dwindling. Only one of us actually has, though. ¶ I don't know why I'm telling you this. It wouldn't make much of a bedtime story.
<!DATALOST!>

MONTH05

My dear one, ¶ They've known. For a while now. ¶ A miscalculation, we've been told, a "minor" one, "but with tragic consequences." Mars, our future there--it's gone. ¶
<ERROR%%> thif fea is a hell of a lot bigger than anything Davy Jonef ever failed<ERROR%%>
All my love-- ¶ ?MISSING?
<!DATALOST!>

MONTH04

My dear one, ¶ Another month gone by. Space travel gets boring after a while. When I was a boy in North Dakota, my dad used to tell me his sea stories from his Navy days. He'd use the same line somewhere in every story: "Being at sea at night is just like being on the prairie." He'd found it comforting, I guess, the big bowl of starry sky over the flat surface of the earth. Whether that surface was water or endless grass didn't matter so much to him. ¶ Later, when I went to sea myself, I learned that for every golden moment of peace mixed with awe, there are hundreds of boring ones to survive. ¶ Now subtract out all the seabirds and dolphins and sunsets, remove the occasional terrifying near-collision with another vessel, and you might begin to understand the monotony of months and months of spaceflight. (Of course, I need to remember that by the time you read this, you'll already be a veteran of interplanetary travel.)
<!DATALOST!>

MONTH03

My dear one, ¶ Something always goes wrong. It can't be helped. Preventative maintenance gets us partway there, but it's not foolproof. ¶ Our first "something" of this particular voyage is a loss of lateral thrusters. As the expression goes, they just shit the bed. (I

know, I'm sorry.) A pretty minor failure, though. They're only used for course corrections, and on a properly planned trip in this day and age there's no usually no need. The statistics are pretty good. They've only been used four times in fifteen trips to Mars, and not at all in the last six voyages. We've got a couple of guys on them trying to get them working again, but no one's too worried. ¶ ?MISSING? habituated to sustained weightlessness, which it seems to me is the biggest perk to space travel. It will be hard to give up flying once we're groundside in a few months. ("Thanks, gravity," he said sarcastically. Although I'll still be pretty bouncy down there. The gravitational field doesn't compare to Earth's.)
<!DATALOST!>

MONTH02
My dear one, ¶ Word came today of your arrival. I spent an uneventful watch staring back at Earth. ¶ It's amazing. Today the planet looks even more beautiful than ever before, even as it is shrinking away to a starry pinprick. I did not think that was possible. ¶ We have slid into routine now. People have their ways of coping: books, movies, working out, doodling. Personally I'm a napper. Have been since my Academy days. The joke back then went like this: if you sleep twelve hours a day, you're only here for two years. ¶ It's true though. Napping is a cheap and restorative form of time travel. ¶ I hope you are sleeping well. Cut that nice lady who's always feeding you a break, will you? ¶ All my love-- ¶ ?MISSING?
<!DATALOST!>

MONTH01
My dear one, ¶ A week or two more and I might have seen you born. But you know, or you will know, how these things are--timed, down to the second--so, I will miss it. Your mother refused to find out your gender (by the time you read this, you'll be fully aware of how stubborn she is), but I know that whether you're ultimately named Jason or Penelope, "my dear one" will apply. ¶ Leaving was made a little easier because I know that God willing we'll all be together in a few years, you, your mother, and me. I know you won't understand some of this stuff for years, but when you're old enough, we'll sit down together and you'll get all this news when it's nothing but history. You'll know then that, even in the midst of the mission, you

were foremost in my mind. ¶ Until that day, your mom will have to let you know how much I love you. ¶ All my love-- ¶ Dad
<BEGIN TRANSMISSION>
<BLASTOFFBLASTOFFBLASTOFF>

AUTHOR BIOGRAPHIES

Jacquelyn Bengfort grew up in a library on the prairie and formerly drove warships for a living. Her work has appeared or is forthcoming in Gargoyle, Midwestern Gothic, Storm Cellar, Noble/Gas Qtrly, CHEAP POP, and District Lines, among other places. A graduate of the U.S. Naval Academy and the University of Oxford, she pays taxes in the District of Columbia and can be found online at www.JaciB.com.

Diana Smith Bolton is the founding editor of District Lit. Her work has appeared in 32 Poems, Beltway Poetry Quarterly, Cactus Heart, Cider Press Review, Coldnoon, Lines + Stars, Punchnel's, The Pedestal, and elsewhere. She earned her MFA at the University of Florida and lives in northern Virginia.

Terri Bruce has been making up adventure stories for as long as she can remember. Like Anne Shirley, she prefers to make people cry rather than laugh, but is happy if she can do either. She produces fantasy and adventure stories from a haunted house in New England where she lives with her husband and three cats. She is the author of two paranormal/contemporary fantasy novels, Hereafter (Afterlife #1) and Thereafter (Afterlife #2), and her short story "The Lady and the Unicorn" will appear in the NH Pulp Fiction "Live Free or Dragons" anthology (Plaidswede Publishing, Fall 2016). Visit her on the web at www.terribruce.net.

Tanya Bryan is a writer living in Toronto, Canada. Her work has appeared in Feathertale Review, Drunk Monkeys, as well as several anthologies. She can be found online at tanyabryan.ca and on Twitter @tanyabryan.

Tara Campbell [www.taracampbell.com] is a Washington, D.C.-based writer of crossover sci-fi. With a BA in English and an MA in German Language and Literature, she has a demonstrated aversion to money and power. Originally from Anchorage, Alaska, Tara has also lived in Oregon, Ohio, New York, Germany and Austria. Her fiction has appeared in the Hogglepot Journal, Lorelei Signal, Punchnel's, GlassFire Magazine, the WiFiles, Silverthought Online, Toasted Cake

Podcast, Litro Magazine, Luna Station Quarterly, Up Do: Flash Fiction by Women Writers, T. Gene Davis's Speculative Blog, Master's Review, Sci-Fi Romance Quarterly, Latchkey Tales, Elementals: Children of Water, and Magical: An Anthology of Fantasy, Fairy Tales, and Other Fiction for Adults.

Marlena Chertock is the Poetry Editor for District Lit and a graduate of the Jiménez-Porter Writers' House. Her poems have appeared or are forthcoming in Lines+Stars, The Little Patuxent Review, Medical Literary Messenger, Fukushima Poetry Anthology, jaffatelaqlam, Crab Fat, Cacti Fur, Straight Forward Poetry, and The Syzygy Poetry Journal. Her articles have appeared in The Washington Post, Marketplace, NBC News, News21, WTOP, USA TODAY, and The Gazette. Find her at marlenachertock.com or @mchertock.

Misha Herwin is a writer of book and short stories for adults, children and young adults. She is fascinated by time and the supernatural and loves creating alternative, magical worlds. In her spare time she is either reading, in her garden, or baking. Muffins are a specialty.

Christina Marie Keller works as a federal editor for Carroll Publishing. Her work has appeared in the anthology Magical: An Anthology of Fantasy, Fairy Tales and Other Magical Fiction. She lives in the Washington, DC area.

Jamie Killen's stories have appeared or are forthcoming in numerous publications including Space and Time, Heiresses of Russ 2013, and Mythic Delirium. She lives in Arizona and blogs at jamieskillen.wordpress.com.

Llanwyre Laish's formative years were filled with the fairy tales and myths of Britain and Ireland. As an adult, she spent nine years sandwiched between gargoyles and rare books, racking up degrees while studying the versions of those tales told in the Middle Ages and the nineteenth century. She now teaches academic writing and writes about roleplaying games.

Kate Lechler is a Visiting Professor of English at University of

Mississippi, where she teaches early British literature and Renaissance drama. She is also a writer and reviewer of speculative fiction; her work has been published in NonBinary Review and is forthcoming in Illumen. She curates a weekly column called "The Expanded Universe" at FantasyLiterature.com, and is currently working on a novel set in a futuristic theme park. She lives in Oxford with her husband, Wil Oakes, a dog, a cat, and seven fish.

Bruce Markuson lives with his wife and two children in Milwaukee WI. and has a number short stories published. Bruce is also working on a number of series. He enjoys writing and often finds himself with writer's obsession. He says the best way to write is to have an ending then write to that ending. Check out his blog at brucemarkuson.blogspot.com.

Gargi Mehra is a software professional by day, a writer by night and a mother at all times. Her short stories and essays have appeared in numerous literary magazines. She blogs at http://gargimehra.wordpress.com/ and tweets as @gargimehra.

Juliana Rew is a software engineer and former science and technical writer for the National Center for Atmospheric Research in Boulder, Colorado. She has sold stories to The Colored Lens, Stupefying Stories, PerihelionSF, and Mad Scientist Journal, among others. Her author website is julianarew.com.

Rafael S.W is a recent Creative Writing graduate and a founding member of Dead Poets' Fight Club. He has been published in The Big Issue Fiction Edition, Voiceworks, and Award Winning Australian Writing. He also regularly contributes to Going Down Swinging online and competes in poetry slams and giant-sized chess games. http://rafaelsw.com

Johnna Schmidt has been the Director of the Jimenez-Porter Writers' House at University of Maryland since 2005. She got her start in writing through an interest in theater, and has performed original work across the U.S., mostly in San Francisco and New York City. She later pursued and received an MFA in Creative Writing: Fiction, at UMD. Her work has been published in Beltway Journal for the Arts, Little Patuxent Review, On the Issues Magazine, and Like Water Burning. Johnna resides in Hyattsville, MD with her husband, two sons, and two dogs.

Tabitha Sin writes speculative fiction and hybrid memoir-fiction. She lives in NYC and thinks about ghosts far too often. Her works have appeared in Side B Magazine, Amok: An Anthology of Asia-Pacific Speculative Fiction, Sonic KCRW: Tracing Love, Moonroots zine, and Thought Catalog. You can follow her on Twitter: @tabithameep.

Sarena Ulibarri earned an MFA from the University of Colorado at Boulder, and attended the Clarion Fantasy and Science Fiction Writers' Workshop in 2014. Her fiction has appeared in Lightspeed, Fantastic Stories of the Imagination, Lakeside Circus, and elsewhere. She is an assistant editor for World Weaver Press and co-editor of the anthology Specter Spectacular III: 13 Uncanny Tales. Find more at sarenaulibarri.com.

Michelle Vider is a writer based in Philadelphia. Her work has appeared in The Toast, The Rumpus, Lady Churchill's Rosebud Wristlet, Atlas and Alice, Baldhip Magazine, and elsewhere. Find her at michellevider.com.

ABOUT THE EDITOR

Kelly Ann Jacobson is a fiction writer and poet who lives in Falls Church, Virginia. She received her MA in Fiction from Johns Hopkins University, and she now works as an Adjunct Professor of Literature and Composition.

Kelly is the author of several published books, including the literary fiction novel *Cairo in White* and *The Troublemakers*, an action-romance. She writes YA fantasy under her pen name, Annabelle Jay. Her work, including her other two anthologies *Magical: An Anthology of Fantasy, Fairy Tales, and Other Magical Fiction for Adults* and *Answers I'll Accept: True Accounts of Online Dating*, can be found at www.kellyannjacobson.com.

47054003R00071

Made in the USA
Lexington, KY
25 November 2015